Aunt Dimity Down Under

ALSO BY NANCY ATHERTON

Aunt Dimity's Death

Aunt Dimity and the Duke

Aunt Dimity's Good Deed

Aunt Dimity Digs In

Aunt Dimity's Christmas

Aunt Dimity Beats the Devil

Aunt Dimity: Detective

Aunt Dimity Takes a Holiday

Aunt Dimity: Snowbound

Aunt Dimity and the Next of Kin

Aunt Dimity and the Deep Blue Sea

Aunt Dimity Goes West

Aunt Dimity: Vampire Hunter

Aunt Dimity Slays the Dragon

Aunt Dimity Down Under

NANCY ATHERTON

VIKING

VIKING
Published by the Penguin Group
Penguin Group (USA) Inc., 375 Hudson Street,
New York, New York 10014, U.S.A.
Penguin Group (Canada), 90 Eglinton Avenue East, Suite 700,
Toronto, Ontario, Canada M4P 2Y3
(a division of Pearson Penguin Canada Inc.)
Penguin Books Ltd, 80 Strand, London WC2R 0RL, England
Penguin Ireland, 25 St. Stephen's Green, Dublin 2, Ireland
(a division of Penguin Books Ltd)
Penguin Books Australia Ltd, 250 Camberwell Road, Camberwell,
Victoria 3124, Australia
(a division of Pearson Australia Group Pty Ltd)
Penguin Books India Pvt Ltd, 11 Community Centre, Panchsheel Park,
New Delhi – 110 017, India
Penguin Group (NZ), 67 Apollo Drive, Rosedale, North Shore 0632,
New Zealand (a division of Pearson New Zealand Ltd)
Penguin Books (South Africa) (Pty) Ltd, 24 Sturdee Avenue,
Rosebank, Johannesburg 2196, South Africa

Penguin Books Ltd, Registered Offices:
80 Strand, London WC2R 0RL, England

First published in 2010 by Viking Penguin,
a member of Penguin Group (USA) Inc.

1 3 5 7 9 10 8 6 4 2

Publisher's Note
This is a work of fiction. Names, characters, places, and incidents either are the product of the author's imagination or are used
fictitiously, and any resemblance to actual persons, living or dead, business establishments, events, or locales is entirely coincidental.

Library of Congress Cataloging-in-Publication Data

Atherton, Nancy.
Aunt Dimity down under / Nancy Atherton.
p. cm.
ISBN 978-0-670-02144-4
1. Dimity, Aunt (Fictitious character)—Fiction. 2. Women detectives—England—Fiction. I. Title.
PS3551.T426A93443 2010
813'.54—dc22   2009040139

Printed in the United States of America
Set in Perpetua
Designed by Alissa Amell

For Vic and Raewyn James,
who took me there and back again

Aunt Dimity Down Under

One

 $\mathcal{I}$ didn't see it coming. As I bustled around my kitchen, making dinner for the men I loved, I didn't see death hovering in the wings. When life is tumbling merrily along, we seldom stop to think about it ending. We ignore the shadow lurking just offstage. Nothing can prepare us for its entrance.

There wasn't a shadow in sight on that golden afternoon in late September. The autumn sun shone benevolently on my dark-haired husband and our equally dark-haired sons as they flew a kite in the back meadow, and a balmy breeze ruffled the snowy locks of my newly retired father-in-law, who sat beneath the apple tree, reading the Sunday *Times*. Life, I thought, as I stirred the pumpkin soup and peeked at the ham baking in the oven, couldn't get much better than this.

My husband, Bill, was tall, good-looking, and as kind as he was wise. Our six-year-old twins, Will and Rob, were happy, healthy, and as bright as buttons. We lived in a honey-colored stone cottage amid the rolling hills and patchwork fields of the Cotswolds, a rural region in England's West Midlands. Although we were Americans, we'd lived in the Cotswolds for nearly a decade. The twins had never known another home.

Bill ran the European branch of his family's venerable Boston law firm from a high-tech office in Finch, the nearest village. When Will and Rob weren't pretending to be dinosaurs or galloping their gray ponies over hill and dale, they attended Morningside School in the nearby market town of Upper Deeping. I looked after my family, helped my neighbors, participated in a plethora of volunteer activities, and ran a charitable foundation called the Westwood Trust.

My father-in-law, William Willis, Sr., had until recently served as the head of Willis & Willis, the family firm. Although he still acted as the firm's chief adviser, the passage of time and a desire to spend more of it with his grandsons had persuaded him to hand the reins of power over to Bill's cousin Timothy Willis. Willis, Sr., would have preferred to pass the reins to his son, but Bill had no interest in power and no intention of uprooting his family for the sake of a prestigious title. Willis, Sr., recognizing that his only child was happier in England than he'd ever be in Boston, had let the matter drop without a word of reproach.

Bill, the twins, and I were actively engaged in a campaign to convince Willis, Sr., to move in with us permanently. We'd transformed our former nanny's room into a cozy but luxurious grandfather's room and we'd tried every trick in the book—including pleading, guilt-tripping, and reasoning—to force him into the bosom of our family.

Our crusade was supported wholeheartedly by a phalanx of plump ladies in Finch, who considered an immaculately tailored, unfailingly polite, and undeniably wealthy widower in his early seventies to be quite a catch. Whether my father-in-law would trade his massive mansion in Boston for a modest cottage in Finch, however, remained to be seen.

Willis, Sr., had arrived at the cottage three days earlier not simply to visit his grandsons, but to attend an event that would take place in Finch on the following Saturday. My bustling came to an abrupt halt as I caught sight of the kitchen calendar and felt my heart swell with anticipatory joy.

In less than a week, the long-awaited fairy-tale wedding of the century—as I'd dubbed it—would take place in St. George's Church. Kit Smith would marry Nell Harris and open a new chapter in the sweetest and most suspense-filled romance I'd ever witnessed. There had been many times over the past seven years when I'd had reason to doubt that the pair would wed, but love had conquered all in the end, as I'd hoped and prayed it would.

I took a special interest in the couple's happiness because Kit Smith was one of my dearest friends and Nell was the stepdaughter of my best friend, Emma Harris, but I wasn't alone in wishing them well. No one with a functioning heart could be untouched by their unique radiance. The good people of Finch understood that the joining of two perfect soul mates was a rare and precious cause for celebration, and proceeded accordingly.

The women rolled up their sleeves and gave the church a hundred-year cleaning. Its leaded windows gleamed, its candlesticks glittered, its altar cloths glowed, and not a speck of dust could be seen on its polished flagstone floor or its splendidly carved wooden pews. The men mowed the churchyard surrounding St. George's, raked its gravel paths, and planted fresh fall flowers on every grave. Mr. Barlow, the local handyman, had taken it upon himself to re-shingle the lych-gate's leaky roof and to give its aging hinges a generous dose of oil, to prevent unseemly squeaking on the big day.

My neighbors had bestowed the same loving care on their own dwelling places and businesses, which had gone from slightly scruffy to sublime. In Bill's words, Finch now looked as if it were posing for the centerfold of a Prettiest Villages calendar.

There'd been a flurry of shopping trips to Upper Deeping as villagers bought or rented their wedding-day finery. After consulting with Nell's father, Derek Harris, Bill and Willis, Sr., had decided to wear their best Savile Row suits. My dress—an emerald-green silk with long sleeves and a sweetheart neckline—had been made in the village by Sally Pyne, the local tea shop owner and seamstress, but I'd bought my hat at a swanky boutique in London. Over the years I'd learned that hats were de rigueur for women attending English weddings. I wouldn't have dreamed of entering St. George's without one.

Finch was, of course, awash in wedding gossip, to which I contributed freely. My neighbors and I chattered endlessly about the flowers, the cake, the music, the ceremony, and the reception, but our most intense speculation was focused squarely on Nell's wedding gown. What would she wear, we wondered? Silk? Satin? Lace? Taffeta? Would the style be classic or modern? What dress, however glorious, could possibly do justice to such an ethereal beauty? Opinions varied, but since Emma Harris was keeping the gown a closely held secret—even from me, her best friend—the rest of us could do nothing but wait and see.

Luckily, Emma couldn't conceal the plans for the reception from me because my sons would be taking part in it. Emma ran the Anscombe Riding Center from the stables of her sprawling home, Anscombe Manor. Kit was the ARC's stable master as well as my sons' riding instructor, and Nell was in charge of the ARC's dressage classes. Since the happy couple's world revolved around horses, it stood to reason that horses would play a central role in their wedding.

Rob and Will, along with other members of the ARC's gymkhana teams, would form a mounted honor guard to accompany the newlyweds' open carriage from St. George's church to the reception at Anscombe Manor. Because each member of the honor guard would be attired in formal riding gear, Emma had been forced to discuss her plans with the participants' parents. Needless to say, I gleefully relayed the insider information to my neighbors as soon as Emma passed it on to me.

The names on the guest list had been broadcast at regular intervals by Peggy Taxman, who, as Finch's postmistress, had personally handled each of the invitations. The guest list had aroused much interest in the village because it included a duke, an earl, several knights, and a retired London police detective as well as a handful of French counts. Friends past and present would walk, ride, fly, drive, and, in once case, pilot a private helicopter to Finch to take part in the joyous occasion.

Emma and Derek Harris had gone to great lengths to prepare Anscombe Manor for the reception. They'd cleaned the great hall from top to bottom, engaged a caterer, hired musicians, brought in professional gardeners to tidy the grounds, and purchased enough champagne to float a battleship. On the morning of the wedding, Derek would rope off a parking area, Emma would put the horses in the pasture farthest from the manor house, and they would both run a brand-new flag up the family's flagpole.

I could hardly wait to see it wave.

The costumes were ready, the stage was set, and the cast was assembling. In less than a week, I told myself, staring dreamily at the cluster of hearts I'd drawn on the kitchen calendar, Kit Smith would finally—*finally!*—marry Nell Harris. My eyes welled with happy tears.

Sighing rapturously, I dried my eyes and turned off the oven. I was about to call my menfolk in to wash up before dinner when the telephone rang. I quickly wiped my hands on my apron and answered it, hoping that another delicious tidbit of gossip would soon be in my keeping.

"Lori?" said Emma Harris.

"Emma!" I replied cheerfully. "How's it going? Have you and Derek finished scrubbing the rhododendrons and vacuuming the lawn? I've been keeping an eagle eye on the weather forecast for Saturday and it looks as though a shower of rose petals will be falling—"

"Lori," Emma interrupted, and it occurred to me that she sounded a bit strained.

"You poor thing," I commiserated. "You must be exhausted. If you need help with anything, and I do mean *anything,* I can be over in two shakes of a pony's tail. Just say the word and I'll—"

"Lori!" Emma exclaimed. "Will you please *shut up?*"

I stared at the telephone in amazement. Emma was a cool, calm, and collected sort of woman. She had never before raised her voice to me and I'd never heard her tell anyone to shut up. The pressure of planning the wedding of the century had clearly gotten to her.

"No problem," I said meekly. "What's up?"

"I don't know how to break it to you gently, so I'll just go ahead and say it," Emma replied tersely. "The wedding's off."

"Good one," I said, chuckling. "You almost sound convincing. Now stop joking around and—"

"I'm not joking," she said heavily. "The wedding has been called off. Nell and Kit have postponed it indefinitely."

"They've . . . they've *what?*" I hunched over the phone, unable to believe my ears. "Are you *serious?* Why in heaven's name would they postpone the wedding?"

"It's Ruth and Louise Pym." Emma took a shaky breath. "They're dying."

A shadow seemed to pass over the sun.

Two

*F*elt as though I'd been kicked in the chest. I stumbled across the room and sank, weak-kneed, onto a chair at the kitchen table. Emma's heart-wrenching news shouldn't have come as a surprise to me, but it had shaken me to the core.

Ruth and Louise Pym were the utterly identical twin daughters of a man who had for many years been the parson at St. George's Church in Finch. The sisters had never married and had spent all of their industrious lives together in their father's thatched, redbrick house on the outskirts of the village. No one knew how old they were, but they were by far the oldest members of our community—most guesses placed them well over the century mark. Although the sisters appeared to be as frail as lace, their energy had always been boundless, their work ethic, awe inspiring. They routinely accomplished more in one day than most women half their age could accomplish in a week.

When Bill and I had moved into the cottage, the Pym sisters had been among the first to welcome us. They'd attended our wedding, embroidered our sons' christening gowns, invited us to countless tea parties, and shared with us their vast store of local lore. Ruth and Louise were keen gardeners, skilled needlewomen, superb cooks, faithful churchgoers, the best of good neighbors, and the only other pair of identical twins Will and Rob had ever met. They were, in short, irreplaceable.

"Ruth and Louise are dying?" I said, half-hoping I'd misunderstood Emma's words. "Are you sure?"

"I'm sure," said Emma.

"How did you find out?" I asked.

"Ruth called me around two o'clock this afternoon to let me know that she and Louise had finished making Nell's veil," Emma said. "The veil was their wedding gift to Nell. They've always been very fond of her." Emma's voice seemed to catch in her throat, but after a short pause she carried on. "To save them the trouble of dropping it off, I drove over to their house to pick it up. When they didn't answer the door, I let myself in."

I nodded. Locked doors were a rarity in Finch. My neighbors considered it perfectly acceptable to enter a house uninvited to do a favor for an absent friend.

"I found the finished veil neatly folded in a cardboard box on the dining room table," Emma went on, "but Ruth and Louise were upstairs in bed. They told me they'd had a funny turn and insisted that there was no need to make a fuss, but I didn't like their color or the way they were breathing, so I telephoned Dr. Finisterre. He came as quickly as he could and it didn't take him long to make a diagnosis. Apparently he's known about their condition for some time."

"What condition?" I asked.

"It's their hearts," said Emma. "They're . . . worn out."

"I don't understand," I said, clutching the telephone with both hands. "They took a train trip to the seaside a couple of weeks ago. How could they make a journey like that if their hearts were weak?"

"Dr. Finisterre advised them not to go," Emma informed me, "but they were convinced that the sea air would do them good, so they went anyway. The doctor believes that the stress of travel brought on the current crisis."

"I would have driven them, if they'd asked," I said softly.

"We all would have," said Emma, "but they didn't ask. They have their pride, I suppose. They're accustomed to looking after themselves."

"It's hard to break the habits of a lifetime," I acknowledged, "especially such a long lifetime. Has the doctor taken them to the hospital?"

"No, they're still at home," Emma said. "They wouldn't let me or Dr. Finisterre call an ambulance for them. They refuse to go to the hospital and I can't say that I blame them. I certainly don't want to end my days hooked up to feeding tubes and monitors."

"Nor do I," I agreed, "but if something can be done to help them . . ."

"Nothing can be done," Emma said with an air of finality. "Dr. Finisterre can make them comfortable, but apart from that . . . It's only a matter of time."

I groaned softly and put a hand to my forehead. "How much longer does Dr. Finisterre think they have?"

"He can't say for certain," Emma answered. "They could last for another six months or they could be gone tomorrow. I broke the news to Nell and Kit as soon as I got back to the manor—about a half hour ago. They immediately decided to put the wedding on hold."

"Naturally," I murmured.

"They're at the Pyms' house now," Emma continued. "I imagine Dr. Finisterre is putting them in the picture as we speak. I've asked him to keep me in the loop. I'll let you know if there are any . . . developments."

"Thanks," I said.

Emma cleared her throat. "I know that we have a lot to talk

about, Lori, but it'll have to wait. Now that the wedding's been postponed, I have a long list of telephone calls to make. The guests, the caterers, the string quartet—"

"I'll make the local calls for you," I offered. "I know every number in Finch by heart."

"Thanks, but I think it would be better if I spoke with everyone personally," said Emma. "I'm the stepmother of the bride. The guests will expect to hear the bad news from me."

"Of course they will," I said. "If I you need help with anything else, or if you just need a break, don't hesitate to call."

"I won't." Emma stopped speaking for a moment. Then she said quietly, "I knew they wouldn't live forever—no one can—but it seemed as though . . ." Her words trailed off.

"I know," I said consolingly. "I can't believe it, either. I guess it'll take a while to sink in."

"I guess so," said Emma. "Well. I'd better start making those phone calls."

"I'm here if you need me," I reiterated. "Any time, night or day."

"I'll be in touch," she said, and hung up.

I laid the phone on the table and stared blankly at the kitchen wall, trying to conceive of a world without the Pym sisters in it. It was like trying to imagine a garden without flowers. I might have sat motionless until nightfall if I hadn't been roused from my reflections by the sound of my husband's voice.

"The ham smells delicious," said Bill, bending to look into the oven. "Do you want me to mash the potatoes?"

I swung around in the chair to look at him and his smile faded abruptly.

"What's wrong, Lori?" he asked, glancing at the abandoned telephone. "Has someone died?"

"Not yet," I said, peering anxiously through the back door. "Where are the boys?"

"In the garden. Father is reading the county cricket scores to them." Bill sat in the chair next to mine and leaned toward me, his elbows on his knees. "What is it, Lori? What's happened?"

"Oh, Bill . . . ," I began, and the whole tragic tale came pouring out. When I'd finished recounting everything Emma had told me, I looked at him helplessly. "How are we going to tell the boys? They *adore* Ruth and Louise. What are we going to say to them?"

"We'll keep it simple," said Bill, "and we'll answer their questions as best we can. They're bound to ask questions. They always do."

"Do you think we should tell them right away?" I asked.

"I don't see how we can avoid it," he replied. "They'll know something's wrong as soon as they see your face. But we don't have to tell them that the Pyms are on their deathbeds. We'll say that they're seriously ill. There's no need for us to cross the final bridge until we come to it." He took me by the hand and got to his feet. "Come on. Let's get it over with."

Will and Rob received the news of the Pyms' illness in thoughtful silence. The questions Bill had predicted didn't start to flow until we were halfway through an unusually solemn dinner.

"Are Miss Ruth and Miss Louise as old as Toby?" Will asked, spearing a green bean with his fork.

Toby was a sweet-natured pony who'd taught dozens of Anscombe Riding Center pupils the rudiments of horsemanship before being put out to pasture at the ripe old age of twenty.

"Miss Ruth and Miss Louise are much older than Toby," Bill replied.

Will nodded and dipped his green bean into his mashed potatoes.

"Toby was sick once," Rob observed, "but he got better. Will Miss Ruth and Miss Louise get better?"

"They might," said Bill.

"What if they don't get better?" asked Rob. "Will they die like Misty's foal?"

A forkful of juicy ham turned to sawdust in my mouth. Misty's foal had died of pneumonia the previous spring. It had been the boys' first direct encounter with death and it had made a big impression on them.

"Yes," Bill said gently. "I'm sorry to say it, sons, but if Miss Ruth and Miss Louise don't get better, they will die."

"I would miss them if they died," said Rob, digging into his applesauce.

"So would I," said Bill, "and so would your mother and your grandfather. We would all miss them very much."

"We should go and see Miss Ruth and Miss Louise before they die," Will decided.

"We will," said Bill, "but not tonight. They need to rest tonight. If Dr. Finisterre says it's all right, we'll go to their house after school tomorrow. Okay?"

"Okay," the boys chorused.

It wasn't until I was tucking the twins into bed that they asked about the wedding. When I informed them that it had been postponed because of the Pym sisters' illness, they gazed reflectively at the ceiling.

"Maybe Nell can make Miss Ruth and Miss Louise better," said Will.

"She made Storm better when he had his cough," Rob reminded me.

Storm, Rob's much-loved gray pony, had come down with a mild case of colic a week ago, from which he had since recovered.

"Nell gave Storm medicine," Rob went on, "and she walked him around and around his stall."

"And he got better," said Will.

"I'm sure that Nell will do everything she can for Miss Ruth and Miss Louise," I said. "But sometimes people die even when you do everything you can for them."

"Like Misty's foal," said Will.

"Like Misty's foal," I confirmed.

"Read us a story, Mummy," Rob said.

I didn't waste time asking for a "please." I simply reached for our copy of *Winnie-the-Pooh* and read it aloud to my little boys, hoping they would drift off to sleep thinking of Tigger and Piglet and Roo rather than Misty's foal.

Bill and Willis, Sr., were in the living room when I came downstairs. No one, it seemed, was ready to go to bed. Bill sat in his favorite armchair with Stanley, our black cat, curled blissfully in his lap. Willis, Sr., stood peering into the darkness beyond the bay window with his back to the room. I sank into a corner of the chintz sofa and gazed into the fire Bill had lit in the hearth after dinner.

"Did they have more questions?" Bill asked.

"They're hoping for a miracle cure from Nell," I replied.

"Aren't we all?" said Bill, stroking Stanley's glossy fur.

Willis, Sr., turned away from the window and crossed to hold his well-manicured hands out to the fire. While Bill and I were clad in blue jeans and wool sweaters, my father-in-law was attired in a three-piece gray suit, a white shirt, and a silk tie. Willis, Sr., hadn't yet gotten the hang of retirement.

"You spoke the simple truth at the dinner table," he said to Bill.

"I will miss the dear ladies most sincerely when they're gone. I've never met anyone else quite like them."

A mischievous memory flitted through my mind and I surprised myself by grinning at my father-in-law. "Do you remember the first time you tried their raspberry cordial?"

"I do indeed." Willis, Sr., smiled ruefully and left the fire to sit in the armchair opposite Bill's. "It sounded like an innocent, wholesome refreshment, but——"

"——it had a kick like an Army mule," Bill put in. "Delectable, but deadly."

"The two of them tossed it back as if it were mother's milk," I marveled.

"Whereas I coughed and sputtered like a badly tuned automobile," said Willis, Sr. "The experience was highly instructive."

"Instructive?" Bill asked. "In what way?"

"It taught me never to underestimate the apparently harmless drinks served by elderly, churchgoing ladies," said Willis, Sr. "Their damson wine was a force to be reckoned with as well. I soon learned to accept nothing but tea from their fair hands."

"And cream cakes," I said.

"And seed cake," Bill added.

"And chocolate eclairs," I went on, "and macaroons and meringues."

"Ah, those excellent meringues . . ." Willis, Sr., heaved a reminiscent sigh.

Our stroll through memory's bakery came to a screeching halt when the telephone rang. Bill answered it and I braced myself for the announcement none of us wanted to hear, but after exchanging a few brief words with the caller, he held the phone out to me.

"It's Kit," he said. "He wants to speak with you."

I jumped to my feet and took the phone from Bill.

"Kit?" I said. "Where are you?"

"Nell and I are still at the Pyms' house," he replied. "I think you should be here, too. Ruth and Louise have been asking for you."

"I'll be there in five minutes," I said. I cut the connection, tossed the telephone to Bill, and headed for the front door.

"Lori?" said Bill, dislodging a reluctant Stanley from his lap and following me into the hallway. "Where are you going?"

"Ruth and Louise are asking for me." I pulled a woolen jacket from the hat rack and thrust my arms into it. "I'll take the Rover."

"Do you want me to drive?" Bill asked.

"I want you to stay here," I said, grabbing my keys from the telephone table, "in case there's more bad news to break to the boys."

I gave him a quick kiss, called good night to Willis, Sr., and sprinted through the crisp night air to our canary-yellow Range Rover. As I turned the key in the ignition and backed the Rover down our graveled drive, I tried in vain to prepare myself for what might be my last visit with the Pyms.

Three

The fields on either side of our narrow, twisting lane were shrouded in darkness and hidden from view by hedgerows, but I was conscious of their presence nonetheless. Harvesttime had come to my corner of the Cotswolds. All too soon, I told myself, the reaper would swing his blade and the ripe sheaves would be gathered.

"Stop being so melodramatic," I muttered irritably as I cruised past Anscombe Manor's winding drive. "The crops around here will be harvested by brawny men in big machines, not by a black-robed skeleton wielding a scythe."

Still, it was hard to ignore the season's symbolism.

I negotiated the lane's most hazardous bend, and the Pym sisters' house came into view, shining like a jewel nestled in velvet. Light poured from each lace-curtained window beneath the shaggy thatch, giving the redbrick walls a mellow glow. I was surprised to see how many lamps were burning in the house—I'd expected it to be as dimly lit as a sick room—until I noticed the vehicles parked on the grassy strip between the lane and the Pyms' front garden. The row of cars told me that Kit Smith and Nell Harris weren't the Pym sisters' only visitors.

Kit's small pickup was there, as were Mr. Barlow's paneled van, the vicar's black BMW, Miranda Morrow's sky-blue Beetle, Sally Pyne's ancient Vauxhall, and the Peacocks' old Renault. I thought I'd received an exclusive invitation to appear at the Pyms' bedsides, but it looked as though I'd have to wait in line.

I parked the Rover behind the vicar's sedan, then made my way through the wrought-iron gate and into the leaf-strewn garden. As I passed the dried flower stalks shivering forlornly in the neglected beds and borders, I wondered who would make the garden bloom again once the Pym sisters were gone. Since the pair had outlived their blood relations, their house would be sold to a stranger. Would the newcomer preserve the old-fashioned plants the sisters had so lovingly tended, or would he dig them up and replace them with a modern, low-maintenance lawn? It hurt my heart to think of plain grass claiming victory over the Pyms' snapdragons, holly-hocks, and sweet peas, so I pushed the unwelcome image to the back of my mind and hurried forward.

I was halfway up the graveled path when the front door opened and a line of villagers spilled onto the front step, with Lilian Bunting, the vicar's scholarly wife, in the lead.

"We're agreed, then," she said, gazing intently at a small notebook she held in one hand. "I'll devise a rota for cooking, shopping, and general housekeeping duties. Mr. Barlow and Derek Harris will keep the house, the shed, the fences, and the garage in good repair. Miranda will look after the garden and Emma Harris will make sure that none of the fruit goes to waste. Peggy Taxman has already volunteered to deliver their mail directly to the house and Jasper Taxman will see to it that their bills are paid on time. My husband will, of course, tend to their spiritual needs."

"I have the easiest job of all, it seems," murmured the vicar.

"You never know," said Mr. Barlow. "Old ladies can be full of surprises."

The rest of the villagers chuckled and a comprehending smile crept across my face. The social machinery that had been set in motion for the wedding of the century had evidently been diverted to the communal mission of caring for the Pyms. While I'd been preoccupied with symbols and hypothetical heartbreaks, my neighbors had concerned themselves with down-to-earth practicalities.

"It looks as though I've missed a committee meeting," I said, striding forward to join the group. "Sign me up for general house-keeping, Lilian. I'm a dab hand with a feather duster."

"Lori!" she exclaimed, looking up from her notebook. "How nice to see you. Our meeting was quite spontaneous, I assure you."

"Emma's phone calls instigated it," Christine Peacock explained. "As soon as she told me about the Pyms, I left Dick to close up the pub and came right over."

"Each of us drove over as soon as we heard the news," said Miranda Morrow. "We wanted Ruth and Louise to know that they're not alone."

"Peggy said we'd only be making a nuisance of ourselves," Sally Pyne noted tartly, "so she and Jasper stayed at the Emporium. If you ask me, she'd rather fill her till than help her friends."

"The Taxmans offered their highly useful services via the tele-phone before Teddy and I left the vicarage," Lilian Bunting pointed out, with a reproving glance at Sally. "I'm sure we're all very grate-ful to them."

"I'm sure we're all very tired and somewhat overwrought," the vicar observed mildly. "It's been a difficult evening. Shall we con-tinue on to our cars? I've no doubt that a good night's sleep will settle our nerves and prepare us for the tasks that lie ahead."

"Ever the voice of reason," said Lilian, smiling at her husband. "You're quite right, Teddy. We've accomplished all we can in a few short hours. It's time for us to leave Ruth and Louise in peace."

I exchanged good nights with the villagers as they left the garden, but as Lilian passed, I touched her sleeve.

"Don't forget to add my name to the rota," I said.

"I've already done so," she said, tapping a fountain pen against the notebook. "I'll let you know when you and your feather duster will be needed."

I waved good-bye to my neighbors as they drove back to Finch, then turned to face the solitary figure standing in the doorway.

Kit Smith smiled wearily at me. He was dressed in faded blue jeans, a dark-blue pullover that seemed to be sprouting bits of hay, and a pair of thick woolen socks. His patched and mud-stained Wellington boots sat beside Nell's on a rubber mat just inside the doorway.

"Lori," he said. "Come in."

I followed him into the foyer. He left me there to hang my coat on the Pyms' coat tree and add my shoes to those on the rubber mat while he circumnavigated the ground floor, turning off lamps as he went. When he returned to the foyer, I peered up at him worriedly. His violet eyes were so breathtakingly beautiful that, if I hadn't known him so well, I might not have noticed how tired they were.

"You poor thing," I said, standing on tiptoe to give him a hug. "You look as though you've been through the wringer."

"It's been quite a day," he acknowledged, returning my hug warmly.

"I'm sorry about the wedding," I said, stepping back from him.

Kit shrugged. "It doesn't matter. The wedding will happen when it happens."

"I know, but all the same . . ." I rubbed his arm sympathetically. "Where's Nell?"

"Upstairs, with Ruth and Louise," he replied. "She's moved into one of the extra bedrooms. She wants to be on hand to nurse them round the clock."

"Shouldn't they have a professional nurse?" I asked.

"They want Nell," he answered.

"Who wouldn't?" I said with a wry smile.

"I've spent the evening fielding visitors," Kit informed me.

"I noticed," I said "Word does travel fast in Finch."

"That it does," he agreed. "The freezer's already filled with the casseroles and soups people have dropped off, not to mention Horace Malvern's cheeses. The rest of the offerings are in here." He led the way into the dining room and began naming the items that littered the long walnut table. "Devotional books from the vicar, chrysanthemums from George Wetherhead, hand-knitted shawls from Sally Pyne, fresh eggs from Mrs. Sciaparelli, honey from Burt Hodge's hives, a packet of Miranda Morrow's herbal remedies, six bottles of Dick Peacock's homemade wine, and a pile of mystery novels from Grant Tavistock and Charles Bellingham."

"I suggest that you pour Dick's wine down the sink," I said. "I'm sure he means well, but——"

"It's not for the faint of heart," Kit put in.

"Or the weak of stomach," I added. I surveyed the villagers' gifts in silence, then said, "It looks as though people are anticipating a prolonged siege. Are they being optimistic?"

"Maybe. Maybe not." Kit ran a hand through his short, prematurely gray hair. "Dr. Finisterre says that his patients have proved him wrong too often for him make predictions."

"I didn't see the doctor's car out front," I said. "Is he still here?"

"No," said Kit. "He showed Nell what to do, then went home. He'll stop by again in the morning." Kit cocked his head toward the hallway. "You'd better go up."

"I've never been upstairs before," I confessed. "Which bedroom is theirs?"

"Turn left at the top of the stairs," said Kit. "Their bedroom is the first one on the left."

"Thanks." I started to leave the dining room, hesitated, and turned back. "Did they really ask for me, Kit?"

"Several times," he replied. "I don't know what's on their minds, but it definitely involves you."

"Maybe it's something to do with the twins," I said, frowning puzzledly.

"There's one way to find out," said Kit with a meaningful look.

"I'm going," I said, and left him gazing at the gifts on the dining room table.

Kit's directions were unnecessary, as it turned out, because Nell was waiting for me at the top of the stairs.

"I heard your voice," she said.

Nell looked more like a fairy princess than a nurse. She was tall and willowy, with golden hair that fell in soft ringlets around a face so exquisite that case-hardened men of the world tended to melt when they caught sight of it. She was dressed, like Kit, in blue jeans, an old pullover, and woolen socks, but she somehow managed to look regal no matter what she was wearing. I couldn't detect the slightest trace of sorrow, regret, or fatigue in her. Her midnight-blue eyes were as serene as ever, and her manner was calm and entirely self-assured. Although Nell was only nineteen years old, she was, and always had been, more mature than I'd ever be.

"I'm sorry about the wedding," I said.

"The wedding will keep," said Nell. "Ruth and Louise won't."

I looked down the darkened hallway. "How are they?"

"They're waiting for you," she said. "I'll be downstairs if you need me. Kit's in desperate need of a cup of cocoa. He's been a bit overwhelmed by well-wishers." She bent to kiss me softly on the cheek, then floated down the stairs as gracefully as an autumn leaf.

I took a steadying breath, walked to the first door on the left, and let myself in to the Pyms' bedroom. The room was just as I'd imagined it would be—spacious, airy, and unmistakably feminine. The ceiling was white and the walls were covered with a pretty wallpaper patterned with pale blue ribbons and bunches of bright red poppies. A wood fire crackled in the tiled fireplace to my left, throwing bright reflections across the polished floorboards.

To my right, a matching pair of white-painted iron beds sat on either side of an oval night table that held two rose-shaded lamps and a pair of well-thumbed Bibles. The bedclothes on each bed were identical, from the crocheted coverlets layered atop the white duvets to the ruffled bed skirts and the lace-edged pillowcases. A splendidly carved oak wardrobe filled the wall next to the doorway, and two white-painted dressing tables sat side by side between a pair of tall windows that overlooked the front garden. The dressing tables held matching silver-backed brushes, yellowing ivory combs, hand-painted porcelain boxes, and delicate bottles filled with the lavender water the sisters made every summer.

The only discordant notes in the room were struck by the medical paraphernalia Dr. Finisterre had left behind. An oxygen tank sat beside each bed, and a card table placed discreetly in a dim corner held medicine bottles, a blood-pressure cuff, and a thermometer. I averted my eyes from the card table and turned to regard the Pyms.

Ruth and Louise sat upright in their beds, propped against piled pillows. They weren't wearing oxygen masks or tubes to help them breathe, so I assumed they weren't in the final throes of their illness. Their long white hair had been loosed from the buns they usually wore and lay fanned across their pillows like bridal veils. They were clad in matching dove-gray bed jackets made of quilted silk and trimmed at neckline and cuff with ivory lace. Their blue-veined hands lay motionless atop the coverlets, but their bright bird's eyes followed me closely as I crossed from the doorway to stand between their beds.

As always, I found it impossible to tell the sisters apart until one of them spoke. Ruth invariably opened our conversations.

"Lori," she said in a weak and breathy voice, "how kind of you . . ."

". . . to visit us at such a late hour." Louise's voice was as faint as her sister's. "We won't . . ."

". . . keep you long," Ruth continued. "Please . . ."

". . . make yourself comfortable," Louise finished.

My throat tightened when I realized how much I would miss the Pyms' ping-pong manner of speaking, but I swallowed my emotions, drew a chair from one of the dressing tables, and took a seat between the beds.

"Rumor has it that you had a funny turn," I said.

"It's only to be expected," said Ruth. "We're not . . ."

". . . spring chickens," said Louise. "I rather think we're . . ."

". . . ready for plucking," said Ruth with a wheezy chuckle.

"I wouldn't put it quite so bluntly," I said, wincing.

"Ah, but we would," Louise pointed out. "There's no need to feel . . ."

". . . sad about our parting, Lori," Ruth went on. "To everything . . ."

". . . there is a season," said Louise. "Our season has been rich and full . . ."

". . . and much longer than most," said Ruth. "My sister and I are almost ready to shuffle off . . ."

To Buffalo? I thought wildly. The plucked-chicken metaphor had thrown me for a loop.

". . . our mortal coils," Louise completed the Shakespearean tag matter-of-factly. "Before we do so, however, we must . . ."

". . . set our affairs in order," said Ruth. "We must . . ."

". . . tie up some loose ends," said Louise. "Unfortunately, we've left it . . ."

". . . a bit late," said Ruth. "We are no longer able to do . . ."

". . . what needs to be done," said Louise.

"We need your help," they chorused.

"I'm yours to command," I said promptly. "Tell me what you want me to do and I'll do it."

The Pyms' voices had been growing steadily weaker and their eyelids were beginning to flutter. I was afraid they would fade into sleep—or worse—without clarifying their request, but they roused themselves sufficiently to manage a few more sentences.

"Aubrey," Ruth said. "Please . . ."

" . . . find Aubrey," said Louise. "Mother and Father will want to know . . ."

". . . what happened to him," Ruth said.

They raised their right hands simultaneously to point at the fireplace.

"Speak to Fortescue," Ruth whispered. "He'll explain . . ."

". . . everything," Louise concluded.

As their hands fell onto the coverlets, identical furrows appeared on their identical brows.

"Don't worry," I told them. "I'll take care of it."

Their brows smoothed, their bright eyes closed, and much to

my relief, their thin chests rose and fell in the regular rhythm of sleep.

"Save your strength," I murmured, looking from one gently wrinkled face to the other. "I'll speak to Fortescue. And I'll find Aubrey for you."

It was a somewhat hollow boast since I had no idea who Fortescue was and I'd never heard of Aubrey, but ignorance had never kept me from taking action. I returned the chair to the dressing table, then went to search the fireplace for clues that might tell me what to do next.

I found one immediately. A business card sat on the mantel-shelf, propped against a charming porcelain tabby cat. Printed on the card in a flowery but legible script were the words:

Fortescue Makepeace, Solicitor
Number Twelve, Fanshaw Crescent
Upper Deeping
(01632) 45561

"The family solicitor?" I murmured, pocketing the card. "I hope Mr. Makepeace knows who the heck Aubrey is."

Even as I spoke, I thought of someone else who might be able to fill me in on the mysterious Aubrey, but to test my hunch, I would have to return to the cottage.

I tiptoed out of the bedroom and crept downstairs as noiselessly as I could. I found Kit and Nell sitting before the fire in the front parlor, sipping cups of hot cocoa. Nell's flawless face was tranquil and Kit's haggard expression had been replaced by one of pure contentment. I hated to intrude on the cozy scene, but I couldn't leave without asking the obvious questions. I motioned for them to keep their seats as I stepped into the room.

"Have the Pyms ever mentioned the name Aubrey to you?" I asked.

"No," said Kit.

"Never," said Nell.

"What about Fortescue Makepeace?" I said.

"He's the family solicitor," said Kit, confirming my guess. "He popped in for a chat with Ruth and Louise shortly after the doctor left."

"How are they?" asked Nell.

"Sleeping," I said. "Which is what I should be doing. Good night, you two. Take care of Ruth and Louise—and each other."

I left the nearly-weds to their vigil and drove away from the Pyms' house, wishing I'd been a fly on the wall when the sisters had had their little chat with Fortescue Makepeace.

Four

The lights in the living room were still lit when I reached the cottage, and the fire was still crackling in the hearth. Bill and Willis, Sr., had waited up for me, though Willis, Sr., had exchanged his three-piece suit and immaculate leather shoes for neatly pressed pajamas, a paisley silk robe, and handmade Italian bedroom slippers. Stanley had apparently been keeping watch at the bay window for my return because he'd moved from Bill's lap to the cushioned window seat, but he'd fallen asleep on duty, curled into a glossy black ball.

While I warmed my hands at the fire, Bill made a cup of chamomile tea to warm the rest of me. I drank it gratefully as I told him and Willis, Sr., about my extraordinary evening at the Pyms'. They were impressed but not surprised by the villagers' spirited response to the tragic situation.

"Your neighbors have always rallied around one another in times of need," said Willis, Sr. "I would have been shocked and dismayed if they'd neglected to do so under the present circumstances."

"Ditto," said Bill. "I'm particularly glad to hear that Nell's there to look after Ruth and Louise. Nell's as capable as any nurse-for-hire and she's always had a special relationship with the Pyms."

"The dear ladies are extremely fond of Eleanor," Willis, Sr., concurred. He was the only person I knew who used Nell's proper name. "I believe her presence will be highly beneficial to them, whatever the eventual outcome."

Neither Bill nor his father had ever heard of Fortescue Makepeace, and the name Aubrey meant nothing to them, but they urged me nonetheless to visit the family solicitor as soon as possible.

"I shall take my grandsons to school tomorrow morning," Willis, Sr., informed me, "and I shall retrieve them after school, leaving you free to confer with Mr. Makepeace."

"My docket's pretty full, but I'll do whatever I can to help," Bill chimed in.

"Wow," I said, beaming at them. "The villagers may not have surprised you, but you've managed to astonish me."

"In what way?" asked Willis, Sr.

"I didn't expect you to be so supportive," I replied. "I thought you'd accuse me of making a promise I couldn't keep and plunging headlong into yet another wild goose chase."

Bill shook his head. "You seem to forget that, as estate attorneys, Father and I have had rather a lot of experience with last wills and testaments."

"A deathbed wish is sacrosanct," Willis, Sr., explained. "Whether you can fulfill it or not is irrelevant. The pursuit is all."

"You may succeed or you may fail," Bill put in, "but you're obliged to try. By the same token, we're obliged to help you. Not that obligation matters in this case. We'll do our best for the Pyms because"—he shrugged—"they're family."

"I couldn't agree more," I said. "Thanks, both of you. With Team Willis behind me, I can't fail."

"And on that hopeful note," said Bill, getting to his feet, "I will bid you good night. I have to be at the office by seven tomorrow for a conference call, so it's time for me to hit the sack."

"I, too, shall retire," said Willis, Sr., rising. "Will and Rob will expect a certain degree of energetic enthusiasm from me on the way to school, and I must not disappoint them."

"Coming, Lori?" said Bill.

"I'll be up in a bit," I replied. "My brain is spinning too fast for sleep right now."

"Don't let it overheat," he said. "You'll need to keep your wits about you when you meet with Fortescue Makepeace."

He bent to kiss the top of my head, then accompanied his father upstairs. Stanley promptly jumped down from the window seat and padded after them, determined, no doubt, to hop into bed with Bill and claim the warm spot behind Bill's knees.

I waited until silence reigned on the second floor, then made a beeline for the study, where I hoped to speak with the one person who might be able to calm my spinning brain. I'd kept mum about my little side trip because, although Willis, Sr., understood many things, I wasn't convinced that he'd understand my relationship with Aunt Dimity.

It was, to be sure, a fairly odd relationship. For one thing, Aunt Dimity wasn't my aunt. For another, she wasn't entirely alive. Since her body had been laid to rest in St. George's graveyard before Bill and I had moved into the cottage, most people would, in fact, describe her as completely dead. But I wasn't one of them.

Dimity Westwood had been born and raised in England. She'd also been my late mother's closest friend. The two women had met in London while serving their respective countries during the Second World War and they'd maintained a steady correspondence long after the guns had fallen silent and my mother had sailed back to America.

To call the pair *pen pals* would be to understate the depth of their friendship. Dimity's letters had helped my mother to recover from my father's early death and to face the subsequent challenges of full-time work and single parenthood. Their lifelong correspondence had provided my mother with an oasis of peace in her unexpectedly chaotic world.

My mother was very protective of her oasis. When I was growing up, I knew Dimity Westwood only as Aunt Dimity, the redoubtable heroine of my favorite bedtime stories. I didn't learn about the real Dimity Westwood until both she and my mother had joined the ranks of the dearly departed. It was then that Dimity had bequeathed to me a comfortable fortune, a honey-colored cottage in the Cotswolds, the letters she and my mother had exchanged, and a curious blue-leather-bound journal.

It was through the blue journal that I finally came to know my benefactress. Whenever I spoke to its blank pages, Aunt Dimity's handwriting would appear, an elegant copperplate taught in the village school at a time when a computer was a clever man who worked with numbers. I'd nearly fainted the first time Aunt Dimity had communed with me from beyond the grave, but I'd long since accepted her as an indispensable presence in my life. I considered myself thrice blessed to call the heroine of my childhood my friend.

The study was dark, but it wasn't silent. A rising wind moaned in the chimney and made the dried strands of ivy rattle insistently against the many-paned window above the old oak desk. I crossed the book-lined room to light the mantelshelf lamps, then knelt to touch a match to the tinder in the hearth. When the wood caught fire, I straightened and looked toward a special niche in the bookcase beside the fireplace.

The niche was occupied by a small rabbit with black button eyes and a pale pink flannel hide. His name was Reginald and he'd been my companion in adventure for as long as I could remember. I never entered the study without greeting him, but tonight's greeting was a somber announcement rather than a cheery "Hello, Reg!"

"The Pym sisters are sick," I said, touching the faded grape juice stain on Reginald's powder-pink snout. "They may not last the night, so I hope you won't mind if I skip the small talk. I need to speak with Aunt Dimity."

Reginald's eyes seemed to gleam solemnly in the firelight, as if he understood the gravity of the situation. I nodded to him, then pulled the blue journal from its shelf and sat in one of the tall leather armchairs facing the fireplace. Instead of opening the journal, however, I rested my hand on its smooth front cover and gazed at the leaping flames.

Until that moment I hadn't considered how difficult it would be to tell Aunt Dimity about the Pyms. The cottage she'd bequeathed to me had been the one in which she'd been born and raised. She'd known Ruth and Louise her entire life. Although she was intimately familiar with death, I wasn't sure how she'd react when I told her that two of her oldest friends were about to join her in the great beyond.

I looked up at Reginald, found strength in his kindly gaze, and opened the journal.

"Dimity?" I said. "I'm afraid I have some sad news to tell you."

I blinked as Aunt Dimity's elegant handwriting swept across the page in a blur of royal-blue ink.

Does it concern Will, Rob, Bill, or William?

"They're fine," I assured her hastily. "So am I and so is Stanley. But Ruth and Louise Pym aren't."

Oh, dear. What has happened to them?

"Their hearts are giving out," I said gently. "Dr. Finisterre doesn't think they have much longer to live. . . ." I went on to tell her about the doctor's diagnosis, the villagers' outpouring of affection, and the postponement of the long-awaited wedding. When I finished, there was an extended pause in which nothing new appeared on the page. Then the handwriting began again, more slowly this time, as if Aunt Dimity were lost in distant memories.

I owe them my life, you know. After Bobby died, I didn't want to go on living.

I stopped breathing for a moment, then leaned closer to the page. Bobby MacLaren had been Aunt Dimity's one true love. He'd been shot down over the English Channel during the Battle of Britain and his body had never been found. She rarely mentioned him.

Ruth and Louise wouldn't let me give in to my grief. They rousted me out of the cottage and put me to work in their vegetable garden. They didn't tell me that life goes on. They let me see it for myself. As I weeded and watered and watched green shoots reach for the sun, I gradually began to blossom again. I've never forgotten the lessons I learned in their garden. And one of those lessons is, of course, that every life comes to an end. So it's their time at last. I can't say that it's unexpected, but it will be very strange to think of Finch without them.

"Yes, it will," I agreed. In a small village, every person counted, but the Pyms counted more than most not only because they were good and decent women, but because they connected Finch to its past in a way no one else could. "The whole village will go into mourning when they die."

I should hope so. But after the mourning, life will go on. I'm glad the boys had a chance to know them. It's fortunate, too, that you've had time to say good-bye to them.

"I hope I have time to do more than that," I said. "They asked me to do a favor for them, Dimity, and I'd really like to do it while they're still around to know that it's been done."

What favor have they asked of you?

"They asked me to find Aubrey," I said.

Aubrey? They asked for Aubrey?

"They asked me to *find* Aubrey," I repeated.

They must have been delirious.

"They didn't seem delirious to me," I said. "To tell you the truth, they seemed remarkably clearheaded."

They couldn't have been clearheaded, Lori, or they wouldn't have asked you to find Aubrey.

"Why not?" I asked.

Because Aubrey can't possibly be alive. He was five years older than Ruth and Louise. He must be dead and buried by now.

"Let's back up a step," I said. "Who *is* Aubrey?"

Didn't they tell you?

"They're as weak as kittens," I explained. "They asked me to find Aubrey, then drifted off to sleep before they could give me further details."

Vagueness was ever their hallmark, bless them. Very well, then, I'll tell you what I know. Ruth and Louise weren't the only children in the Pym family. There was a boy as well. Aubrey Jeremiah Pym was the Pym sisters' older brother.

"I didn't know they had a brother," I said, frowning.

Few people do. I never met Aubrey, but I heard stories about him when I was a little girl, whispers shared by grown-ups when good children were supposed to be in bed.

"What kind of stories?" I asked.

The kind that surface in the wake of a family tragedy. Aubrey wasn't a nice young man, Lori. In fact, he was a scoundrel.

I leaned back in the chair and gazed skeptically at the journal. In my experience, whispering villagers favored highly colored rumors over the plain, unvarnished truth. Aunt Dimity might take the old, overheard stories seriously, but I found it almost impossible to believe that the genteel, hymn-singing Pym sisters could be related to a scoundrel.

"Aubrey was a bad boy, was he?" I said, raising an eyebrow. "What did he do? Leave the house without a clean pocket handkerchief?"

Your customary flippancy is unwarranted in this case, Lori. Aubrey Pym was a disgraceful reprobate. His beleaguered parents could do nothing to stop his gambling, his drinking, his womanizing, and his fighting, but when he took money from the poor box to pay for his vices, they were forced to act. The poor box he emptied, I might add, was the one in St. George's Church.

"The son of a parson robbed a poor box to pay for his betting and boozing?" I said, appalled.

He did. My father was strolling past St. George's on the night in question. He caught young Aubrey red-handed.

I ducked my head, chastened. "Sorry about the flippancy, Dimity. I should have known that you wouldn't trash a man's reputation without being sure of your facts."

Yes, my dear, you should have.

"Aubrey was a rat, all right," I conceded humbly. "Was he arrested for stealing the money?"

No. His parents couldn't bear the shame of seeing their only son sent to prison, so they covered up the crime. When he refused to change his ways or to show any sign of remorse, however, he was summarily banished from the family home.

"Banished?" I said.

He was sent away with little more than the clothes on his back. The servants were instructed to bar the door to him, his belongings were given to the poor, and he was cut out of his father's will. To my knowledge, none of the remaining family members ever spoke his name again. They certainly did not do so in public.

"What happened to him?" I asked.

No one knows. He was never seen again in Finch.

"How old was Aubrey when his parents gave him the boot?" I asked.

He'd just turned twenty.

"Good grief." I said, taken aback. "He must have started down the wrong path at an early age."

He broke his parents' hearts, Lori. They were never the same after Aubrey left. My father believed that they blamed themselves for their son's wickedness, but I suspect that they regretted their decision to banish him. I think they must have longed for a reconciliation that never took place.

"Loose ends," I murmured, nodding. "Ruth and Louise told me that their mother and father would want to know what happened to Aubrey."

I imagine they already know what happened to him, since he's surely as dead as they are.

"Why are you so certain that he's dead?" I asked. "If Ruth and Louise are anything to go by, the Pyms are a long-lived family."

Long-lived, perhaps, but not immortal. Do you honestly believe that a man who lived as carelessly as Aubrey could outlive Ruth and Louise?

I had to admit that Aunt Dimity had a point. Men who drank, gambled, fought, slept around, and took things that didn't belong to them stood a better than average chance of dying young. Nevertheless, I didn't think the Pyms would have asked me to achieve the impossible. I drummed my fingers on the arm of the chair while I turned the matter over in my mind.

"Maybe they want me to find Aubrey's grave," I said finally. "It might give them some peace of mind to know where he's buried. Scoundrel or not, he was their big brother."

He was an unrepentant villain, but I know what you mean. Time has a way of softening harsh memories. If you've interpreted the Pyms' wishes correctly, how do you propose to find Aubrey's grave?

"I'll start by speaking with their family solicitor," I replied. "I intend to meet with him tomorrow. His name is Fortescue Makepeace, his office is in Upper Deeping, and Ruth and Louise promised that he would explain everything."

I hope he will.

"I hope he has a map with a big red *X* on it," I said, "marking the spot where Aubrey is buried."

I wouldn't be quite that hopeful. But I'm sure that Mr. Makepeace will be as helpful as he can be. Have Bill and William voiced their opinions on your latest venture?

"They're behind me one hundred percent," I said.

As am I, my dear.

"I never doubted it." I smiled briefly, then gazed pensively into the fire. "The Pyms have entrusted me with what feels like a huge responsibility, Dimity. Why do you suppose they picked me?"

I can think of several reasons, but you cited the most important one. The Pyms trust you, Lori. They know that you won't rest until you've carried out their wishes. They selected you because you're demanding, tenacious, and inquisitive.

"In other words," I said dryly, "I'm bossy, bullheaded, and nosy."

You have a host of qualities the Pyms admire, my dear. They are depending on you to use those qualities to fulfill their last request.

"I'll give it my best shot," I said. "But will it be good enough? What if they die before I find Aubrey's grave?"

You mustn't allow "what-ifs" to discourage you, Lori. Where there's life, there's hope, and the Pyms are—for the moment, at least—still very much alive. Cast aside your doubts and fears and get on with the task at hand.

"Easier said than done," I murmured.

Most things are. I have faith in you, Lori. I'm certain that you will be able to locate Aubrey's grave. I would suggest, however, that you get some sleep before you start looking for it. Old graves aren't as easy to find as you might think. You'll need to be well rested if you're to contend with brambles, wasps' nests, and mud.

"I'll let you know what I find out from Mr. Makepeace," I said.

I look forward to hearing each and every detail. Good night, my dear.

"Good night, Dimity," I said.

I waited until the curving lines of royal-blue ink had faded from the page, then closed the journal and returned it to its spot on the bookshelves. Reginald beamed down at me encouragingly as I knelt to bank the fire.

"Brambles, wasps' nests, and mud won't slow me down," I told him, with more confidence than I felt. "If I have to, I'll go to the ends of the earth to keep my promise to the Pyms."

Had I known what the future held in store for me, I might have chosen my words more carefully. Instead, I patted Reginald's powder-pink snout, turned out the lights, and made my way quietly to bed, where I lay awake for a long time, contemplating life and death and the love of two frail sisters for a banished scoundrel.

Five

ill was gone before dawn the following morning. I rose early enough to see him off, but I didn't linger on the doorstep because the weather had taken a decided turn for the worse. The wind had continued to rise throughout the night, bringing with it a cold, driving rain that lashed the windows and transformed the graveled drive into a short but challenging run of rapids. It felt as though Mother Nature were railing against the Pym sisters' demise, but a telephone call to Nell assured me that such objections were premature. Ruth and Louise had requested tea and toast for breakfast and were resting comfortably, despite the storm.

Since it was still too early to wake the twins, I went upstairs to change out of my flannel nightie and into an ensemble I deemed suitable for my meeting with Mr. Makepeace. I wanted him to regard me as a serious person, capable of carrying out whatever task the Pyms had set for me, but I also wanted to keep warm, so I selected a gray cashmere sweater, black wool trousers, and a pair of black leather boots that would stand up to a bit of mud.

By the time I finished dressing, Will and Rob were up. I helped them to don their school uniforms and brushed their hair, then herded them downstairs to the kitchen for sustaining bowls of hot porridge slathered with cream and sprinkled with chopped dates. Willis, Sr., joined us a few minutes later, wearing a tweed suit and his sturdiest brogues.

"I see that you've dressed for the weather," I commented as I ladled porridge into his bowl and mine. "There's a definite nip in the air and it's raining sideways. It seems more like late October than late September. Are you sure you want to take the boys to school?"

"I am," he replied. "Tempests hold no fear for me, Lori. Apart from that, I'd rather be of service than spend the day counting raindrops."

"Do you count raindrops, Grandpa?" Will asked interestedly.

"Not often," Willis, Sr., replied.

"You'd have to count fast," Rob observed.

"And know big numbers," Will added. "Bigger than a hundred million."

"Bigger than a hundred million *billion*," Rob countered.

While my sons continued their scholarly analysis of raindrop-counting, I gave my father-in-law a thoughtful glance. His comment about wanting to be of service had given me a new and potentially useful idea. It stood to reason that a man accustomed to running a busy law firm would find idleness unappealing. Perhaps, I told myself as I put the saucepan in the sink, the best way to persuade Willis, Sr., to move in with us permanently would be to provide him with meaningful work.

"Since you're undaunted by the tempest," I said, sitting across from him, "would you mind doing another favor for me? I'm supposed to be in Oxford at ten o'clock, to attend a board meeting for the Westwood Trust. I was going to beg off, but if you could—"

"Consider it done," he said, with a nonchalant wave of his spoon. "I will gladly take your place at the board meeting. Will there be time to discuss the agenda before the boys and I depart?"

I gave him a quick rundown of the board's most pressing business, signed a proxy letter that would allow him to make decisions in my absence, and fetched my briefcase from the study while he and the twins donned their rain gear in the front hall. As Willis, Sr., took the briefcase in his gloved hand he seemed to stand a little taller than he had since he'd first announced his retirement.

"If you require assistance in dealing with Mr. Makepeace, please do not hesitate to summon me," he said, patting the pocket in which he kept his cell phone. "I am considered by some to be fairly fluent in the language of law."

"You're way too modest to be a big-shot lawyer," I said, kissing him on the cheek. "But I'll call you if I need you."

I watched from the doorway while the trio splashed their way down the flagstone path to the Range Rover. After Willis, Sr., had strapped Rob and Will into their safety seats, I waved good-bye to them and retreated to the kitchen to feed Stanley, load the dishwasher, and wipe the table.

It seemed reasonable to assume that a provincial lawyer would be at his desk by nine o'clock on a Monday morning, so when the appointed hour arrived I reached for the telephone and dialed the number engraved on the business card I'd found on the Pyms' mantelshelf. The woman who answered spoke with a lilting Scottish accent.

"Good morning," she said. "You've reached the office of Fortescue Makepeace. Mrs. Abercrombie speaking. How may I help you?"

"Good morning, Mrs. Abercrombie," I said. "My name is Lori Shepherd and I—"

"Ah, Ms. Shepherd," she broke in. "Please forgive the interruption, but Mr. Makepeace advised me that you would be ringing the office this morning on a matter of some urgency. Will it be convenient for you to meet with Mr. Makepeace today?"

"I can be there in an hour," I said, adding thirty minutes to the journey because of the wet roads.

"I shall inform Mr. Makepeace," said Mrs. Abercrombie. "We will expect you at ten o'clock, Ms. Shepherd."

"See you then," I said, and hung up.

I was relieved to hear that the Pyms had paved the way for me with their solicitor. I didn't want to waste time explaining who I was and why I needed to speak with him. Although I appreciated Aunt Dimity's optimism, I wasn't as sure as she was that time was on my side.

"The sooner he tells me what I need to know, the better," I murmured as I headed for the front hall.

I pulled on a voluminous black raincoat that I hoped would withstand brambles and wasp attacks, slung my shoulder bag over my shoulder, and took my keys from the telephone table. After calling good-bye to Stanley, I ran through the pouring rain to my Morris Mini. With luck, I thought, I'd be standing over Aubrey's grave before Rob and Will were out of school.

Number Twelve, Fanshaw Crescent, turned out to be the center section of a three-story Georgian row house located a few blocks south of the marketplace in Upper Deeping. If the sun had been shining, I would have paused to admire the building's gracious, cream-colored facade, but since a frigid monsoon seemed to be in progress, I maneuvered the Mini into a nearby parking space, then made a mad dash for Number Twelve's shiny black door.

I'd scarcely removed my finger from the brass doorbell when the door was opened by a tall, gray-haired woman wearing a tweed skirt, a white blouse, a bulky, oatmeal-colored cardigan, and low-heeled black pumps. She exuded an air of quiet competence as she ushered me across the threshold and relieved me of my dripping raincoat, which she hung in a small room off the foyer.

The woman introduced herself as Mrs. Abercrombie, Mr. Makepeace's secretary, then led me up a curving flight of stone stairs to a pair of double doors that opened onto the second-floor landing. She knocked twice and the doors were opened by a short, round, pink-faced man whose sober black suit was brightened considerably by a white silk waistcoat embroidered with sprays of springtime flowers. What was left of his white hair was combed neatly back on both sides of his otherwise bald head, and he wore a gorgeous yellow orchid in his lapel. His eyes were bright blue and twinkling.

"Your ten o'clock appointment has arrived, Mr. Makepeace," murmured Mrs. Abercrombie.

"I beg your pardon, Mrs. Abercrombie," Mr. Makepeace protested, gazing jovially at me. "This is not my ten o'clock appointment. This is the delightfully obliging Ms. Shepherd, whose willingness to help her neighbors is so far beyond commendable that I scarcely have words to describe it. Do come in, dear lady, and take a seat near the fire. Tea, please, Mrs. Abercrombie, and some of your delicious biscuits. Our guest will be in need of sustenance after her trying journey."

While he spoke, Mr. Makepeace escorted me to a plum-colored Regency chair, one of a pair flanking the rosewood settee that faced the gold-veined white marble fireplace in which a coal fire was burning merrily. The solicitor's office, like his attire, was at once brightly colored and exceptionally elegant. The ceiling was covered with ornate plasterwork, the tall windows were draped in a pale peach brocade, and the settee was upholstered in lemon-yellow silk.

After I'd taken my seat, Mr. Makepeace bustled over to the satinwood desk that sat before the windows. He returned to the fireside clutching a slim, black leather document case, lowered himself into the chair opposite mine, placed the document case on a mahogany table at his elbow, and leaned forward to peer at me imploringly.

"I do apologize for asking you to leave the comforts of your home and hearth on such an insalubrious day, Ms. Shepherd," he said. "My health, alas, is not what it once was, and my doctors discourage me from indulging in unnecessary travel when the weather is disagreeable."

"It was no trouble at all," I assured him. "I don't mind a little rain."

"A *little* rain?" Mr. Makepeace chuckled heartily. "My clients described you as a stalwart soul, Ms. Shepherd, and I can see that they were quite correct. Ah, Mrs. Abercrombie . . ." He looked up as his secretary entered the room carrying a tea tray laden with cups, saucers, a pot of fragrant jasmine tea, and a plateful of what appeared to be shortbread cookies. She deposited the gleaming tray on the mahogany table, then withdrew.

"I've asked Mrs. Abercrombie to hold my calls," Mr. Makepeace informed me. "I am at your service, Ms. Shepherd, for the rest of the morning—for the rest of the day, if need be."

My host poured the tea and proffered the cookies, then waited until I'd had a sip and a nibble before finally getting down to business. I was relieved. Although it was undeniably pleasant to bask in the warmth of a well-stoked fire while bone-chilling bullets of rain hammered the windowpanes, I hadn't braved the storm for the sole purpose of sampling Mrs. Abercrombie's shortbread.

"I believe my clients discussed with you the, er, commission they wish you to undertake," he said.

"I wouldn't call it a discussion," I said with a wry smile. "Ruth and Louise asked me to find someone named Aubrey, told me that you would explain everything, then went to sleep."

Mr. Makepeace twinkled at me genially. "My family has served the Pyms for more than a century, Ms. Shepherd. I'm quite familiar with their little ways."

"So . . . can you?" I asked. "Explain everything, I mean."

"If I could, I would not require your help, dear lady," he replied. "I can, however, impart to you some background information that I believe you will find useful as you move forward in your, um, mission."

He drained his teacup, patted his lips delicately with a linen napkin, returned cup and napkin to the tray, sat back comfortably in his chair, and folded his dimpled hands across his remarkable waistcoat. As I watched him settle in for what appeared to be the long haul, my hopes for acquiring a map marked with a big red *X* began to fade.

"The first thing you must understand, Ms. Shepherd, is that there is more than one Aubrey Pym," he said. "Aubrey Jeremiah Pym, Senior, was my clients' brother. He left England at the age of twenty. At the commencement of the Great War, he volunteered to serve in the armed forces. He died on the sixth of May, 1915, during the Gallipoli campaign."

"Gallipoli?" I said, nonplussed. "Ruth and Louise want me to go to *Gallipoli*? I don't even know where Gallipoli *is*."

"Gallipoli is in Turkey, Ms. Shepherd," Mr. Makepeace informed me, "but I must confess that I have no idea why you would wish to go there."

"I'm supposed to find their brother's grave," I explained, adding uncertainly, "aren't I?"

"Ah." Mr. Makepeace's blue eyes lost some of their twinkle. "I should perhaps explain that Aubrey Pym's death was not . . . tidy. He was, lamentably, blown to bits during an artillery barrage." The solicitor cleared his throat. "He has no grave."

"No, I suppose he wouldn't." I allowed a moment of silence to pass, out of deference to the dead, then pressed on. "I assume, then, that Ruth and Louise were talking about *another* Aubrey. You said there was more than one."

"So I did," Mr. Makepeace acknowledged. "The second Aubrey was the son of the first." The solicitor clasped his hands together and smiled at me. "My clients respectfully request that you, Ms. Shepherd, attempt to establish a direct line of communication between them and their nephew, Mr. Aubrey Jeremiah Pym, *Junior.*"

"I see, I said, nodding. "Would you happen to know where Aubrey Pym, Junior, might be?"

"Indeed, I would," Mr. Makepeace said cheerfully. "My clients have given me permission to furnish you with Mr. Pym's last known address."

I squinted at him in confusion. "If you have his address, Mr. Makepeace, why haven't you contacted him already?"

"I've tried, dear lady." He sighed heavily. "Believe me, I've tried. Much to my dismay, Mr. Pym has failed to respond to my letters. I can think of several reasons for his silence—the address may be out of date, for example, or he may be out of town—but the only way to know for certain is to send a personal representative to find him and to speak with him directly. Hence my need for your services."

"But . . . why bother with letters?" I asked, baffled. "Why don't you just march up to his front door and knock on it?"

"His front door is, alas, beyond my reach," Mr. Makepeace answered. "It is, most unfortunately, located in Auckland, New Zealand."

"New Zealand?" I echoed.

"New Zealand," he confirmed.

"Oh." I cocked my head to one side and peered at him question-ingly. "New Zealand is . . . pretty far away from here, isn't it?"

"It is approximately one thousand miles southeast of Australia," Mr. Makepeace explained helpfully.

"New Zealand is a thousand miles southeast of *Australia*?" I said, my voice rising to a squeak.

"It's down under Down Under," he told me, chuckling happily at his own wit.

I was too stunned to chuckle. I'd come to Upper Deeping fully prepared to spend a day, or perhaps a few days, squelching through muddy graveyards in search of an obscure headstone. Neither Aunt Dimity nor I had considered the possibility of leaving England, not to mention the Northern Hemisphere, in order to track down a live human being.

"Let me get this straight," I said, eyeing Mr. Makepeace doubt-fully. "Ruth and Louise want me to go to New Zealand to find their nephew?"

"Correct," he confirmed.

"Why can't *you* go?" I demanded. "You're their solicitor. Isn't it your job to find long-lost family members?"

"I would go if I could," Mr. Makepeace assured me, "but my health will not permit me to make the journey." He patted his chest. "High blood pressure, you know, and a touch of diabetes. My doctors have advised me most strongly to avoid prolonged flights."

"You could hire a private detective," I suggested, adding with a perplexed frown, "Do they have private detectives in New Zealand?"

"I'm quite certain they do," said Mr. Makepeace, "but my clients do not wish to entrust such a delicate mission to a stranger."

"What's so delicate about finding someone's nephew?" I asked.

Mr. Makepeace drummed his fingers on his waistcoat and regarded me levelly. "Family affairs are often fraught with difficulty, Ms. Shepherd, and my clients' situation is more difficult than most. I'm sorry to say it, but their late brother was not a shining example of British manhood. He was, in fact, a bit of a black sheep. He left England because his involvement in a series of regrettable incidents created a deep rift between himself and the rest of his family."

I had to credit the solicitor with a high degree of tact. According to Aunt Dimity, Aubrey Pym, Sr., had been an unrepentant wastrel who'd been disinherited, disowned, and cast out in disgrace. She would have been dumbfounded to hear him described as "a bit of a black sheep" whose behavior had been merely "regrettable."

"The rift was never bridged," Mr. Makepeace continued. "My clients were forbidden to communicate with their brother in any way. They were informed of his death, of course, but they were unaware of their nephew's existence until ten days ago, when they discovered a letter buried at the bottom of a trunk that had once belonged to their mother."

"Who wrote the letter?" I asked.

"Aubrey, Senior," the solicitor replied. "He wished to inform his mother of his son's birth. I do not know whether she wrote back to him, but I do know that she concealed the letter and the information it contained from her daughters." Mr. Makepeace touched a finger to the orchid in his lapel, then pursed his lips and raised his eyebrows meaningfully. "As I indicated earlier, Ms. Shepherd, the family rift was quite deep."

"What a stupid waste of energy," I said, shaking my head in disgust. "Ruth and Louise would have made wonderful aunts."

"I'm afraid it is too late for them to establish a long-term relationship with their nephew," Mr. Makepeace said softly. "But it is not yet too late for them to reach out to him. They must move cautiously, however, because they do not know how their overtures will be received. It is entirely possible that their nephew is unaware of *their* existence. It is also possible that his mind has been poisoned against them. Their intentions must, therefore, be conveyed with the utmost diplomacy."

I couldn't restrain a snort of laughter. I'd been called many things in my life, but I'd never been called diplomatic. I lost my temper too easily, I spoke too hastily, and I seldom let facts complicate a good theory. If Ruth and Louise expected me to act the part of a discreet, mild-mannered envoy, they'd made a grave error in judgment. An ambassador blessed with my diplomatic skills would be more likely to inflame their family feud than to douse it.

"I'm sorry, Mr. Makepeace," I said, disguising my laughter with a cough, "but I don't think I'm the right person for the job."

"I beg to differ, dear lady," he said, smiling broadly. "My clients regard you as the perfect person for the job. They believe that you will succeed where others might fail because you are"—he closed his eyes briefly, as if he were trying to recall the Pyms' exact words—"strong-willed, determined, and naturally inquisitive."

"Bossy, bullheaded, and nosy," I said under my breath.

"I beg your pardon?" said the solicitor.

"Never mind," I said, motioning for him to go on.

"I have been given to understand that you are independently wealthy," he said. "If such is the case, you will be able to make the journey without risking a loss of income or requiring a leave of absence from your employer."

"I don't work for a living," I conceded, "but I have two young sons and a husband who travels a lot, so I don't see how I can——"

Mr. Makepeace held up a chubby finger for silence.

"My clients," he continued, "believe that your father-in-law, who currently resides with you, will not only be capable of looking after your sons, but glad of the opportunity to do so."

"My father-in-law is great with the boys," I acknowledged, "but he doesn't know the first thing about cooking, cleaning, or doing laundry, so——"

"My clients," Mr. Makepeace broke in, "have informed me that your father-in-law's, er, legions of admirers will, without hesitation, rise to the occasion. I have been advised that the, ahem, merry widows of Finch—my clients' phrase, not mine," he hastened to assure me, "will vie for the privilege of providing your family with the home comforts to which they have become accustomed."

I pursed my lips. If I knew the merry widows of Finch—and I did—they'd provide my family with comforts usually found in five-star hotels. The cottage would be scoured daily, the laundry would be washed by hand, and my menfolk would be fed so many delectable dishes that they'd never again be satisfied by my cooking.

"Your expenses," Mr. Makepeace concluded, "will, of course, be paid in full."

"It's not a question of money," I said, waving the concern aside. "I have responsibilities at home, Mr. Makepeace. I can't drop everything and run halfway around the world on a whim. My family needs me."

The round-faced solicitor leaned forward and gazed at me with a new sobriety.

"You would not be making the journey on a whim," he said quietly. "You would be fulfilling the deepest desire of my clients' hearts. They wish to communicate with their only remaining blood relative before they die. They hope to heal the breach that sundered them from him before it is too late. Ruth and Louise need you, too, Ms. Shepherd. I would argue that their need is greater than your family's."

I felt as if he'd thrust a knife into my heart.

"I'll have to talk it over with my husband and sons," I mumbled, gazing at the floor.

"Naturally," said Mr. Makepeace. "But please do so quickly. My clients may not have much time left." He picked up the black leather document case and handed it to me. "My clients have authorized me to present you with papers giving you the power to act as their legal representative in this matter, Ms. Shepherd. They have also written a letter to their nephew, which they hope you will deliver to him personally. Mrs. Abercrombie will, if you wish, make your travel arrangements. We need but a moment's notice."

I slipped the document case into my shoulder bag and told Mr. Makepeace that I would give him my decision by the end of the day. He thanked me for my time and walked with me to the double doors. I was about to step onto the landing when I paused to look up at him.

"The letter Ruth and Louise found—the one their brother wrote to their mother," I said. "It must have given their hearts a jolt."

"It did," said Mr. Makepeace. "But if you can find their nephew, you may, perhaps, give their hearts ease."

It wasn't until I started up the Mini that I remembered the rash vow I'd made the night before. Never in my wildest dreams had I imagined that I'd be called upon to keep it, yet it seemed that I would, in fact, have to travel to the ends of the earth in order to keep my promise to the Pyms.

That I would make the journey was a foregone conclusion—I could almost feel Bill's hand on the small of my back as he pushed me out of the cottage and hear Willis, Sr.'s voice as he urged me to do my duty—but I wouldn't travel alone.

"I hope you're up for a trip, Dimity," I muttered, "because it looks as though you and I are going to New Zealand."

Six

Some time later, I watched Auckland's bright carpet of lights emerge from the black immensity of the Tasman Sea.

"At last," I muttered hoarsely.

I had no idea how many days had passed since Bill had dropped me off at Heathrow Airport. According to my itinerary, I'd spent twenty-three hours crossing the Atlantic Ocean, the North American continent, and the Pacific Ocean, and an additional four hours killing time during a layover in Los Angeles, but I'd somehow lost two days when I'd crossed the International Date Line, so my sense of time was completely out of whack. I *felt* as if I'd spent most of my adult life confined to the first-class cabin of an Air New Zealand jet. I shuddered to think of what the journey had been like for those traveling in coach.

I turned away from my window to gaze blearily at the smiling face of Serena, my smartly dressed and much too chipper flight attendant. Her clear eyes and glowing complexion brought back distant memories of what it had once been like to be freshly bathed, well-rested, and alert.

"It's five twenty A.M. local time, and we're about to land in New Zealand's largest city," Serena informed me. "If you include the suburbs, Auckland covers sixty square kilometers—that's twenty-three square miles to you Americans—and it contains nearly a third of New Zealand's entire population. Auckland was named after Lord Auckland, the Governor-General of India. It was once the capital of New Zealand, and it's ringed by forty-eight extinct volcanoes."

"Volcanoes?" I said, roused from my torpor.

"*Extinct* volcanoes," said Serena. "The *active* volcanoes are far-ther south."

"How much farther?" I demanded.

"Let's prepare for landing, shall we?" she asked, and moved on to her next victim.

I raised my seat back to its upright and locked position, then turned to gaze downward again. I hadn't expected New Zealand's largest city to be quite so large. Its glimmering lights seemed to go on forever and a surprising number of them seemed to belong to tall buildings. As the plane descended smoothly toward the run-way, I couldn't help wondering if it was safe to build skyscrapers in a city ringed by forty-eight allegedly extinct volcanoes. In my frag-ile, sleep-deprived state, I was a bit put out with everyone who'd had a hand in sending me to a place that might blow itself up with-out warning.

The family conference had gone exactly as I'd predicted. After I'd revealed the true nature of the Pym sisters' request, Bill had pulled my suitcases down from the attic and Willis, Sr., had used the world atlas to show Will and Rob where Mummy would be going. There'd been no debate about whether I *should* go or not. My loved ones had simply assumed that I would leave as soon as possible.

A phone call to Mrs. Abercrombie had put me on the first flight out of London the following morning. I'd been so busy packing, fussing over the boys, making to-do lists for Willis, Sr., and con-ferring with Aunt Dimity that I hadn't had a moment to spare for a last-minute visit with the Pyms. I'd had to settle instead for a hur-ried telephone conversation with Nell, who'd assured me that Ruth and Louise were doing as well as could be expected.

Bill had arranged via e-mail for one of his old school friends—a native New Zealander named Cameron Mackenzie—to meet me at the Auckland Airport and drive me to my hotel, which turned out to be a very good idea. By the time I exited the plane, retrieved my luggage, and passed through the customs and quarantine checkpoints, I could scarcely remember how to summon a taxi, let alone how to give directions to a driver, but thanks to Bill's foresight, I didn't have to fend for myself. I was simply scooped up at the arrivals barrier by a tall, soft-spoken blur of a man who guided me gently to a car and didn't argue with me when I refused to relinquish my carry-on bag to him.

I conked out before he finished putting my suitcase in the trunk and came to when he shook me firmly by the shoulder.

"We're here," he said.

At least, that's what I thought he said. To my sleep-clogged ears, it sounded more like "Weah-heah."

"Okay," I said.

I dragged myself, my shoulder bag, and my carry-on out of the car and allowed the tall blur to lead me into the brightly lit lobby of the Spencer on Byron Hotel, check me in, and board an elevator with me.

"Who are you?" I asked stupidly, peering up at the tall blur.

"Cameron Mackenzie," he replied. "I'm an old friend of your husband's."

"That's right." I nodded groggily. "Do you know what day it is?"

The corners of his mouth seemed to twitch, as if he were suppressing a smile.

"It's Thursday," he said.

"Is it?" My attention wandered to the flashing floor numbers on the elevator's control panel. "Are we in a skyscraper?"

"A small one," he said. "The Spencer has twenty-three floors."

"Will it fall over when the volcanoes erupt?" I asked.

"If the volcanoes erupt, everything will fall over," he answered. "But I wouldn't worry about it. The active volcanoes are—"

"—farther south," I finished for him. "How much farther?"

"Far enough," he said.

"Do you know why I'm here?" I asked, as the elevator doors slid open.

"Bill filled me in," he said, steering me into the corridor. "We don't have to discuss it now, though. You need some sleep."

"I *do*," I agreed fervently.

With Cameron's help, my luggage and I made it to my suite. He deposited my suitcase on a luggage rack in the sitting room, then slipped something into my shoulder bag.

"I've written my room number on the back of my card," he said. "I'm three doors down. Give me a call after you've caught up with yourself."

"Okey-dokey," I said.

Cameron left and I crawled into bed, still clutching my carry-on bag.

I passed the next two hours in blissful oblivion, then woke with a start, wondering where Bill was, why I'd gone to bed fully dressed, and if Cameron Mackenzie had been a figment of my imagination. After I'd unraveled those mysteries, I sat up in bed, reached for the telephone, and called Bill. I didn't know what time it was in England and I didn't care. I needed to hear my husband's voice.

"Did I wake you?" I asked when he answered.

"No," he replied, "but it wouldn't matter if you had. For future reference, Lori, London is twelve hours behind Auckland. How was the trip?"

"Don't ask," I said, stifling a yawn. "How are Ruth and Louise?"

"A little better," Bill replied. "Nell said they perked up when she told them what you were doing. They requested porridge for breakfast, in addition to their usual tea and toast."

"Wonderful," I said.

"Cameron called to let me know you'd arrived," Bill went on. "He said you seemed pretty jet-lagged."

"I think I drooled in his car," I confessed guiltily.

"He won't mind," Bill assured me. "I've asked him to look after you while you're there, so if you need anything, ask him. Have you mapped out a plan for the day?"

"After I hand the Pyms' letter to Aubrey Pym, Junior, I intend to come back to the hotel and sleep until it's time to fly home," I said.

"You'd better get going, then," he advised. "I'll talk to you later."

"Kiss the boys for me," I said. "And tell William I miss him."

"I will," Bill promised, and rang off.

A wave of homesickness threatened to engulf me as I hung up the phone. I kept it at bay by opening my carry-on bag and peering down at a small, powder-pink flannel face. Reginald was used to traveling with me. He was my own personal cure for homesickness.

"You have no idea how good it is to see you, Reg," I said.

I stroked his hand-sewn whiskers fondly and placed him on my bedside table, then withdrew the blue journal from the carry-on and opened it.

"Dimity?" I said. "Weah-heah."

I leaned back against my pillows as the familiar lines of royal-blue ink scrolled gracefully across the page.

I beg your pardon?

"We're here," I said, reverting to my native tongue. "We're in Auckland. It's bigger than Upper Deeping."

I suspected that it might be. How do you feel, my dear?

"Not too bad," I said. "My brain's a little disjointed, but I think I can take a shower without drowning."

Did you read up on your destination during your flights?

"I didn't bring a guidebook with me, Dimity. I won't be here long enough to need one." I looked at Reginald and sighed wistfully. "I'd planned to get my hair cut this week, not circle the globe."

Do try to cheer up, Lori. I, for one, am delighted to be here. I've always wanted to visit New Zealand. I wish we could stay long enough to explore the North Island as well as the South Island, and everything in between. The Maori name for New Zealand is Aotearoa, or Land of the Long White Cloud. Such a poetic image. The correct pronunciation of Maori, by the way, is "Mow-ree," with the accent on the first syllable.

"Hold on," I said, struggling to keep up. "Who are the Maori?"

The Maori are the modern-day descendants of New Zealand's original, Polynesian settlers. Europeans didn't come into the picture until 1642, when two Dutch ships sailed into Golden Bay. A Dutch cartographer christened their discovery New Zealand, after a Dutch province. It didn't become an English colony until 1840.

I gaped at the journal in astonishment. "When did you become an expert on New Zealand?

I met quite a few Kiwis in London during the war. Did you know that New Zealanders are called Kiwis because of the kiwi, a flightless bird unique to New Zealand?

"Everyone knows about kiwis," I said dismissively. "Did you know"—I searched my mind for a handy factoid, to prove that I wasn't a complete ignoramus—"that Auckland was named after Lord Auckland, the Governor-General of India?" I finished triumphantly.

I did. The soldiers I met were very proud of their homeland. They made it sound as if it had everything one could want in a small country— long stretches of unspoiled coastline, snowcapped mountains, tropical jungles . . .

"I'm afraid we won't have much time for sightseeing," I said firmly. "I plan to keep my promise to the Pyms, then catch the first flight back to England."

Of course. The ghost of a sigh seemed to pass through the room, as if Aunt Dimity were already regretting our swift departure. *How do you intend to get to Aubrey Pym's place of residence? It's unwise to drive a rental car when one's brain is disjointed.*

"I won't have to drive," I told her. "I have a chauffeur. His name is Cameron Mackenzie. He's a Kiwi, but he went to school with Bill, back in the States. Bill asked him to keep an eye on me while I'm here."

Excellent. There's nothing quite so useful as a native guide. It's a pity you won't be able to utilize his services to explore the country more fully, but I understand your desire to return to your family.

"My family isn't the only reason I want to go home." I paused for a moment, then gave voice to a concern that had been troubling me. "What if I never see Ruth and Louise again, Dimity? What if they die while I'm here?"

Try not to worry overmuch about losing Ruth and Louise, Lori.

"Dr. Finisterre said—"

Aunt Dimity's handwriting sped across the page before I could complete the sentence.

If you'll recall correctly, Dr. Finisterre refused to say how much time the Pyms have left, and he was right to do so. Ruth and Louise have always been much sturdier than they seem. I believe that they will live as long as they need to live, and they need to live long enough to see their family made whole again. In my humble and thoroughly nonmedical opinion, your search for Aubrey will be the very thing that tethers them to life. It is time, therefore, for you to stop fretting and start moving. Ruth and Louise are counting on you!

A genuine smile curved my lips as the lines of royal-blue ink disappeared from the page. With a few well-chosen words, Aunt Dimity had laid to rest any lingering doubts I'd had about my unexpected journey.

"Hang in there, Ruth and Louise," I murmured, and returned the journal to my bag.

I met Cameron Mackenzie in the lobby an hour later. A hot shower and a room-service breakfast had cleared the cobwebs from my mind, so I was able to see him clearly for the first time. I liked what I saw. He was tall, broad-shouldered, and lean, with short-cropped salt-and-pepper hair, gray eyes, and a mouth that seemed to curve readily into a smile. His weathered face suggested that he spent a lot of time in the great outdoors, but whether for work or for play it was too soon to tell. He was dressed casually, in khaki trousers and a loose-fitting white cotton shirt, but his clothes weren't cheap. If he worked outdoors, I thought, it was by choice, not by necessity.

"*Kia ora,*" he said, extending his hand to shake mine.

"Excuse me?" I said blankly.

"*Kia ora,*" he repeated. "It's a Maori phrase. A literal translation would be: 'I wish you good health,' but people use it for all sorts of things nowadays: hello, good-bye, good luck, cheers, welcome. In this instance, it means: Welcome to New Zealand, Lori! I welcomed you at the airport, but I don't think it registered."

"Sorry about that," I said, ducking my head sheepishly.

"I've seen worse." He pulled a shiny blue cell phone and a charger out of his pocket and handed them to me. "I meant to give these to you at the airport, but I forgot. You can use the phone to call England. My number's already programmed into it."

"Thanks." I slipped his gifts into my shoulder bag and smiled up at him. "For everything, I mean. It's lucky for me that that you and my husband are such good friends."

"Bill's the best," said Cameron. "I'd walk through fire for him."

"I hope helping me will be less painful," I said.

"I'm sure it will," he said, laughing. He motioned toward the lobby's glass doors. "I had them bring the car around. If you're ready, we can be on our way."

"Do you know where we're going?" I inquired.

He nodded. "Bill gave me the address. It's right here, in Takapuna. That's why I booked our rooms in the Spencer."

"Takapuna?" I said, frowning. "I thought we were in Auckland."

"Not quite. Technically, we're in a suburb of North Shore City." Cameron raised his hand and pointed to his right. "Auckland's over there, across Waitemata Harbor."

"*Kia ora,* Takapuna, Waitemata . . ." I sighed. "Just when I'm getting used to your accent, you ambush me with words I can hardly pronounce. I'm a stranger in a strange land, Cameron. I thought New Zealand would be more . . . English."

"New Zealand is many things," he said. "I wish you could stay long enough to see all of it, but Bill told me you were in a hurry to get home."

"I am." I patted the black leather document case in my shoulder bag. "But first I have to deliver a letter. Let's go."

I put on my sunglasses as we stepped out of the lobby. The sun shone brightly in a flawless blue sky, and the air was soft, moist, and scented with salt and seaweed—a reminder of how close we were to the ocean. Across the street from the Spencer, a large but tasteful sign marked the entrance to the Takapuna Lawn Bowling Club. The sign seemed to combine the Englishness I'd expected with the touch of "otherness" I'd found.

"What a lovely day," I said, remembering the frigid monsoon that had drenched me in Upper Deeping.

"Enjoy it while you can," Cameron cautioned. "It's early spring in the Southern Hemisphere. The weather can—and will—change on a dime. Here we are," he added, unlocking the doors of a spotless silver Ford Falcon. "It's a rental. My own vehicle isn't quite as clean."

As we took our respective places in the car, I noted that the steering wheel was on the right-hand side—just like in England. I opened the window to enjoy the balmy breezes while we waited for a group of chattering passengers to board a minivan parked directly in front of us. Undismayed by the delay, Cameron turned to reach for something in the backseat and, much to my surprise, presented me with a colorful cookie tin.

"Anzac biscuits," he said. "Baked by my wife, Donna. 'Anzac' stands for Australian and New Zealand Army Corps. Legend has it that the biscuits were invented during the First World War by women who wanted to send nutritious and durable treats to their men fighting overseas. It's Donna's way of welcoming foreign visitors."

"Your wife is very kind," I said. "Please thank her for me. Do you have children?"

"Two boys," he replied. "They're not twins, like Will and Rob, but they're only a year apart. Braden is ten and Ben is eleven."

"Where do you live?" I asked.

"Near Wellington," he replied. "I'd be more specific, but I don't want your eyes to glaze over."

I smiled ruefully but pressed on. "What job am I tearing you away from?"

"I train horses," said Cameron, confirming my hunch about the outdoorsy nature of his occupation. "And you're not tearing me away from anything. According to my wife, I'm in dire need of a holiday."

"It's a good thing I didn't bring my sons with me," I said. "They'd want you to go back to work straightaway. They love horses."

"I know," he said. "Bill has e-mailed quite a few pictures of Will and Rob on their ponies."

"He's a proud papa," I acknowledged. I looked down at the biscuit tin and shook my head. "I don't know what to say, Cameron. Not every man would leave his wife, his children, and his job for the sake of an old friend."

"Nor would every woman. Looks as though we have something in common." The minivan pulled away and he turned the key in the ignition. "All set?"

"Drive on," I said.

Two minutes later we were cruising down the main drag of a bustling shopping district. Most of the shops were small and independently owned rather than links in multinational chains, and the sidewalks were crowded with people of all ages and races. There was so much to look at that I felt a small twinge of regret when the shops petered out and we entered a residential area.

A left-hand turn took us onto a short street lined with a mixture of fairly impressive mansions and modest but well-tended homes. At the end of the street, I caught a glimpse of ocean framed by towering trees I didn't recognize.

"Pohutukawa trees," said Cameron, following my gaze.

"Pohutu—what?" I said.

"Pohutukawas," he said. "They're covered in red blossoms at Christmastime. Very cheerful."

"Pohutukawa," I repeated carefully, filing the word away for future reference. I planned to spring it on Aunt Dimity when the opportunity arose.

Cameron slowed to a crawl, then parked before a two story house that was modest but not well tended. The top story was clad in corrugated iron siding, the bottom in a pale yellow stucco striped with rust stains. The narrow balcony that ran across the front of the house was littered with cigarette butts and a few leggy plants, and a broken picnic table graced the balding front lawn. Two of the second-floor windows were open, but the windows on the first floor were tightly shut and covered with drapes.

"This is it," Cameron said.

Weah-heah, I thought, and got out of the car.

Seven

Cameron accompanied me to the yellow house's recessed front door and stood a few steps behind me as I pressed a finger to the doorbell. When a voice shouted down to us, we exchanged puzzled glances, then returned to the front lawn, to peer up at the balcony.

A woman gazed down at us through a haze of cigarette smoke. She was clad in a shocking pink T-shirt, cutoff denim shorts, and neon-green flip-flops. Her coarse black hair sprouted from the top of her head in a ponytail drawn so tautly against her scalp that she shouldn't have been able to lower her overplucked eyebrows. Though she dressed like a teenager, her hair was liberally streaked with gray and her blunt-featured face was mottled with age spots. Her voice was deep, gravelly, and loud enough to be heard back at the Spencer.

"What do you want?" she bellowed.

"Good morning," I called up to her. "I'm looking for Mr. Aubrey Jeremiah Pym, Junior. I believe he lives here."

"Not anymore he doesn't," said the woman. "A. J. died two months ago."

"He's . . . dead?" I said, thunderstruck.

"As a doornail." The woman paused to exchange a few pleasantries with a man who'd stepped out of the house next door. The smile that wreathed her face while she spoke to him vanished abruptly when she returned her attention to me. "Who are you, anyway?"

"I'm . . . I'm a friend of the family's," I stammered, still shaken by the news of Aubrey's death.

"A friend of the family's?" She sucked on her cigarette and exhaled a long stream of smoke. "Didn't know they had friends."

"They?" Cameron said alertly. "Does another family member live here?"

"Ed's been sponging off of his dad for years," she said with a contemptuous sneer. "Edmund Hillary Pym, named after our great national hero, the man who conquered Everest." She laughed harshly. "The only mountain Ed Pym ever climbed was a mountain of stubbies."

"Stubbies?" I said to Cameron.

"Beer bottles," he explained.

"What did you want with A. J.?" the woman inquired.

"I had private business to discuss with him." I hesitated, then made a quick decision. The letter I'd come so far to deliver couldn't be read by a dead man, but it could be read by his son. With a half glance at Cameron, I called to the woman, "My business involves Edmund Pym as well."

"If Ed's come into a fortune, you can share it with me," she said, her eyes narrowing. "I'm his landlady. He owes me a month's rent."

"Can you tell us where we might find Ed?" Cameron asked, picking up on my cue.

"Hospital," grunted the landlady. "If he croaks, I'm selling his stuff, to make up for what he owes me. Not that there's much worth selling." She began raking her fingers through her ridiculous ponytail. "Probably end up donating the lot to an op shop. I'll have to clear the place out for my next lodger, won't I?"

"Op shop?" I murmured.

"Opportunity shop," Cameron translated. "A thrift store." He looked up at the landlady. "Which hospital is Edmund Pym in?"

"North Shore," she replied. "If you see him, tell him I want my rent." Smoke curled from her nostrils as she watched a blue Honda park behind Cameron's Ford. "Who's this? Another family friend?"

A woman as tall as Cameron and several times his width got out of the Honda cradling a large manila envelope in her arms. Her short, light-brown hair gleamed in the sunlight and she was neatly dressed in a brown suede jacket, a black V-neck knit top, and flowing black knit trousers. She had a no-nonsense air about her, but her brown eyes seemed kindly behind her boxy black glasses. She paused on the sidewalk to survey our curious gathering, then strode across the lawn with a sense of purpose.

"I beg your pardon," she said, talking to me and to Cameron. Her voice was soft, her manner, pleasantly professional. "My name is Bridgette Burkhoffer and I work for North Shore Hospital. I'm looking for Aubrey Pym. Have I found the correct address?"

"You're in the right place, dear," shouted the landlady, who'd leaned over the balcony's railing to catch the new arrival's every word. "But A. J.'s dead. You should know. He died in North Shore two months ago."

Bridgette favored the landlady with a coldly clinical gaze. "If you wish to speak with me, please come downstairs. I'm not accustomed to raising my voice in public."

"All right, all right, keep your shirt on, Bridge, I'm coming," said the landlady. She took a last drag on her cigarette, crushed the butt beneath her flip-flop, and disappeared from the balcony. A moment later, she came around the side of the house to join us on the lawn.

"Separate entrance," she explained. Though she was now standing face-to-face with the rest of us, she still spoke in an ear-bruising bellow. "My lodgers use the front door." She held out a nicotine-stained hand to Bridgette. "Call me Jessie, Bridge."

"You may call me Ms. Burkhoffer, Jessie," Bridgette said crisply, ignoring the hand. "For your information, Jessie, I am fully aware that Mr. Aubrey Jeremiah Pym, Junior—also known as A. J.—passed away in our hospital two months ago. Clearly, I do not wish to speak with him. I wish to speak with his granddaughter, Miss Aubrey Aroha Pym."

"His granddaughter?" I said, my eyes widening.

"Why didn't you tell us about his granddaughter?" Cameron demanded, rounding on the landlady.

"You wanted to know who lives here," she said defensively. "Bree stuck around long enough to put her granddad in the ground, then grabbed her backpack and hightailed it out of here. Haven't seen hide nor hair of her for six weeks."

Bridgette pursed her lips and turned to me. "May I ask what your relationship is to the Pyms?"

"I'm a legal representative of the Pym family," I replied.

"You told me you were a friend," said Jessie, scowling. "You didn't say anything about being a legal representative." She presented her yellowing palm to me. "Eight hundred dollars or I throw Ed's stuff into the street."

Before I could respond, Cameron pulled his wallet out of his pocket and began counting colorful bills into Jessie's outstretched hand. When he reached three hundred dollars, my jaw dropped. When he added another hundred, I felt I should object.

"Cameron," I said, "there's no need to—"

"Leave it to me, Lori," he interrupted tersely. He shoved the wallet back into his pocket and fixed the landlady with a steely gaze. "I'll send you a check for the balance. If you have any doubts about my character, my good friend the police commissioner will vouch for me." He leaned closer to her and went on in a silky purr that was far more intimidating than Jessie's shouting had been. "And if you remove so much as a scrap of paper from the flat, the commissioner will take time out of his busy schedule to arrest you personally." He stood up straight and snapped his fingers impatiently. "Now give us the key and go away."

Jessie was smart enough to know when she was beaten. She eyed Cameron resentfully, but fished a brass key out of her pocket and handed it to him. Grumbling irritably—and audibly—she retreated around the side of the house.

Bridgette released a pent breath and bestowed a shy smile on Cameron.

"I can't tell you how thoroughly I detest being called *Bridge,*" she said. "*You* may call me Bridgette."

"Thank you, said Cameron. "I'm Cameron Mackenzie and this is my friend Lori Shepherd."

"Pleased to meet you," said Bridgette.

I smiled vaguely in her direction, but I couldn't stop thinking about the Pyms' landlady.

"She didn't even ask us for identification," I said incredulously. "For all she knows, we could be drug dealers setting up a crack house."

"I don't think she'd mind, as long as we paid the rent on time," said Cameron.

"Do you really know the police commissioner?" Bridgette asked.

"I do," he replied. "I taught his granddaughter to ride and I trained his grandson's gelding."

"Why did you pay any rent at all?" I asked, ignoring the digression. "We don't need access to the apartment. We can visit Edmund Pym at the hospital."

"About Edmund Pym . . ." Bridgette cleared her throat. "I hope you won't mind, Ms. Shepherd, but I *would* like to see your identification."

Since I wanted to hear what she had to say about Edmund Pym, I took the document case from my purse and handed her the papers Mr. Makepeace had drawn up for me. I didn't know if their contents would apply to a different set of Pyms, but Bridgette seemed to think that everything was in order. She returned the document case to me and regarded me soberly.

"I regret to inform you that Edmund Hillary Pym died at five o'clock this morning," she said. "I came here to deliver the news to his next of kin, but—"

"She ran away six weeks ago," I said.

Bridgette nodded. "I'm not sure what to do next. No funeral arrangements have been made, you see, and I don't know how to contact Ed's daughter, to find out what her wishes might be."

"Was Edmund Pym married?" asked Cameron.

"His marriage ended many years ago," said Bridgette. "Ed lost track of his wife after the divorce and he had no idea how to get in touch with her at this late date." She shifted the manila envelope in her arms and frowned pensively. "He didn't tell me that his daughter had abandoned him. He kept saying that Bree would come to see him the next day, and the next, but . . . Bree never came."

"It sounds as though you spent a lot of time with him," I observed.

"I'm a critical care nurse," she said. "I try to spend as much time as I can with each of my patients. I was with Ed when he died this morning."

"I'm sorry," I said, with a sympathetic nod. "I'm sure you were a great comfort to him."

"His daughter would have been a greater comfort," Bridgette remarked.

"Did Ed tell you anything else about her?" Cameron asked.

"He told me that Bree's middle name—Aroha—is the Maori word for *love*," Bridgette answered, her expression softening. "He said that she'd turned eighteen recently. Last night, he asked me to tell her that he was sorry."

"For what?" I asked.

"For drinking himself to death, I imagine," she replied. "Pneumonia killed A. J., but his son succumbed to alcoholic cirrhosis of the liver. It wasn't the first time we'd seen Ed at North Shore, but it was the first time he'd been in the critical care unit. A. J.'s death set the stage for Ed's final, fatal binge." She glanced at her watch. "Forgive me, but I must get back to work. I'm already late for my next shift."

"What will you do with Ed's body?" I asked.

"We'll hold it until we run out of room in the morgue," said Bridgette. "If no one claims it by then, we'll bury it in the public cemetery."

"What about his personal effects?" asked Cameron.

Bridgette held up the manilla envelope. "I brought them with me, to give to his daughter, but now . . ."

"We'd be happy to give them to her, when we find her," said Cameron.

"Thank you, but personal effects can be released only to the next of kin." Bridgette shifted the envelope to the crook of her arm, pulled a card out of her jacket pocket, and handed it to Cameron. "I'd be grateful to you if you'd give her my card. I need to hear from her as soon as possible."

"We'll let her know," he said, tucking the card into my shoulder bag.

Bridgette thanked us again, then hastened back to her car and drove off. I turned to stare at Cameron.

"I'm all for the grand gesture," I said, "but have you lost your mind? First you shovel money into the hands of that loudmouthed harpy. Then you promise Nurse Bridgette that you'll find Edmund Pym's daughter. What on earth do you think you're doing?"

"I'm helping you to deliver the letter you traveled eighteen thousand kilometers to deliver," he replied.

"I traveled eighteen thousand kilometers?" I said faintly.

"Bill told me you weren't the sort of woman who lets her friends down," Cameron continued, as if I hadn't spoken. "I assumed, therefore, that you'd want to go after Bree Pym, and I can't let you run around New Zealand on your own. You're a stranger in a strange land, remember? You don't know a takahe from a huhu grub." He cocked his head to one side. "Was I wrong? Would you prefer to tell your friends that their last hope of reuniting their family fizzled because you didn't even try to find their great-grandniece?"

"No," I said uncertainly. "But how are we going to track down an eighteen-year-old girl who left home six weeks ago?"

"We start," said Cameron, "by searching her flat."

As he fitted the key into the lock, I began to suspect that Cameron Mackenzie could teach me a thing or two about being bossy, bullheaded, and nosy.

Eight

"We can't search the flat," I protested. "We'll be arrested for trespassing."

"Only if someone calls the police," Cameron said. "I won't call them, and I think I bought the landlady's silence." He raised a quizzical eyebrow. "Are you going to turn us in?"

"Very funny," I retorted. "But now that you mention it . . . Why not call the police? They'll find Bree a lot faster than we will."

"They won't even look for her," said Cameron. "Legally, Bree Pym is an adult. As far as the police are concerned, she's free to come and go as she pleases. Unless we find evidence to suggest that she was kidnapped, they'll have no reason to look for her." He shook his head. "I'm sorry, Lori, but if we want to find Edmund Pym's daughter, we'll have to do it without help from the authorities."

He turned the key in the lock and tried to open the door, but he had to put his shoulder to it before it would open wide enough for him to slip inside.

"Coming?" he said.

"In a minute," I replied.

I waited on the doorstep until he vanished from view, then took the shiny blue cell phone from my bag and dialed my husband's number. He answered on the first ring.

"Bill?" I said softly, in case the horrible landlady had returned to her perch on the balcony.

"What's up, Lori?" he said.

"I'm at Aubrey Pym, Junior's place," I said. "He's dead. So's his son, Edmund."

"I'm sorry to hear it," said Bill, "but Ruth and Louise will be much sorrier." He sighed. "It looks as though your first day in New Zealand will be your last."

"Not necessarily," I said. "Edmund Pym had a daughter. She's still alive, apparently."

"Apparently?" said Bill.

"She left home six weeks ago," I said. "Cameron thinks we should track her down."

"What do you think?" Bill asked.

"I think Cameron's completely daffy," I replied. "But I also think he's right."

"He usually is," said Bill, chuckling. "Trust Cameron, Lori. If he believes he can find the girl, he probably can. And don't worry about me or the boys or Father. I know you'll find it hard to believe, my love, but we can survive without you for a few more days."

"I'll bet Sally Pyne is washing your father's socks in rose water," I grumbled.

"We miss you, too, Lori," Bill soothed. "I'll let Ruth and Louise know what's going on."

"Tell them that their great-grandniece's name is Aubrey Aroha Pym," I said urgently. "Tell them that Aroha is the Maori word for *love*."

"I'll tell them," Bill assured me. "Keep me posted."

"Will do," I said, and cut the connection.

I dropped the phone into my shoulder bag, took a deep breath, and entered the last known residence of Aubrey Jeremiah Pym, Jr. A deep breath was needed because the place reeked of stale beer, unwashed laundry, and spoiled food. After stepping around the scattered mound of mail that had blocked the front door, I went directly to a window, threw back the drapes, and cranked it open. The salty breeze that ruffled my dark, curly hair helped to dissipate the fug.

"Good idea," Cameron said from the living room. "Wish I'd thought of it myself."

The apartment had an open floor plan. A breakfast bar separated the kitchen from a small dining area, where I stood, and nothing separated the dining area from the rectangular living room.

"Now we know why no one replied to Fortescue Makepeace's letters," I said, nodding toward the toppled pile of bills, circulars, and assorted envelopes near the front door. "It looks as though the mail hasn't been touched for weeks."

Cameron nodded. "Ed must have been either too drunk or too ill to deal with it."

The apartment's furnishings were pitiful: a beat-up wooden table with four rickety chairs, a sagging sofa, an aged television set, an oversized recliner with ragged holes in its cheap leather uphol-stery, and a modern blond brick fireplace grimed with thick layers of soot. Fast-food wrappers, pizza boxes, and empty beer bottles littered the floor. The slovenly flat bore no resemblance whatsoever to the Pym sisters' immaculate house.

A faded afghan covered the back of the recliner and a soiled pillow lay crumpled beneath a threadbare woolen blanket on the sofa. It wasn't hard to picture a sick old man watching television from the chair while his drunken son sprawled uselessly on the couch. How, I wondered, did Bree fit into the picture?

"I don't know why they stayed on in Takapuna," Cameron commented. "They could've found a cheaper flat in Auckland. It looks as though they spent every penny they earned on rent."

"Not much worth selling," I murmured.

"Not much," he agreed. "But a few things." He pointed to six photographs standing in tarnished frames on the concrete mantelshelf. "Some of the frames are solid silver, to judge by the weight. Why didn't the family sell them? They could have used the extra cash."

"The pictures must have meant something to them," I reasoned, "frames and all."

I crossed the room, carefully avoiding the beer bottles in my path, and picked up what seemed to be the oldest photograph. The sepia-toned wedding portrait had been taken in a studio, before a painted backdrop depicting a garden in the midst of Grecian ruins. The bride and groom were decked out in the height of Edwardian fashion. The bride's wasp-waisted gown appeared to be made out of satin with lace panels, a fringed bodice, and elaborate beading. The groom was formally attired in a top hat and morning dress.

The young woman was conventionally pretty, but the young man was downright dashing. A signet ring glinted from his right pinky finger and a half dozen fobs dangled from the watch chain spanning his waistcoat. I couldn't tell whether he was smiling or not, because his mouth was obscured by a handlebar mustache, but his dark eyes seemed to be laughing.

I turned the picture over and saw handwriting on the back.

" 'Ten June 1912,' " I read aloud. " 'Mother and Father, on their wedding day.' " I examined the photo again. " 'Father' must be Aubrey Pym, Senior—my friends' banished brother. He left England around 1910, so the date works."

"Looks like he married money," Cameron said, eyeing the photograph shrewdly.

"He had a way with women," I acknowledged. "It's one of the reasons his father banished him."

"I'd say he landed on his feet." Cameron picked up a very old black-and-white photograph. In it, the mustachioed man stood in the arched entryway of a large church, holding a chubby-cheeked, lace-bedecked baby in his arms. Cameron flipped the picture over and read aloud, " 'Twenty-seven April 1913, Aubrey and A. J. at ChristChurch Cathedral, Christchurch. Baptism.' "

"Baptism?" I echoed puzzledly. "Where's A. J.'s mother? No mother would miss her child's baptism."

Cameron pointed to a black armband on the sleeve of Aubrey, Sr.'s well-tailored overcoat. "Died in childbirth?"

I took the photograph from him and studied it closely. Aubrey, Sr.'s face was gaunter than it had been in the wedding portrait, and the laughter had left his eyes.

"I think you're right," I said slowly. "Poor A. J. I don't know if Bill mentioned it to you, Cameron, but Aubrey, Senior, was killed in 1915, at Gallipoli. If his wife died in childbirth, it means that A. J. lost both of his parents before he was three years old."

"Poor little guy," Cameron murmured.

"I wonder what happened to him after his parents were gone?" I said. "How did he go from the doors of ChristChurch Cathedral to a rundown dump in Takapuna?"

"Will answering those questions help us to find Bree?" Cameron asked.

"It might help us to understand her, once we find her," I replied. "And I'd like to be able to tell Ruth and Louise something about their family, even if we don't find Bree."

We looked at the rest of the photographs. A black-and-white snapshot of a young man in a World War II uniform revealed that A. J., like his father, had served in the armed forces. Unlike his father, however, A. J. had been fortunate enough to return from the battlefield. A second wedding portrait told us that he'd married late in life, and that his wedding had been a much more humble affair than his father's. The bride wore a plain white blazer and skirt, the groom, a dark suit, and they stood before the blank background of an inexpensive photography studio.

A. J.'s son, Edmund, showed up only once, in a family photo taken on the shores of a steaming lake. In it, Ed, his wife, and their little girl seemed to radiate happiness.

" 'Twenty-seven February 1985, Ed, Amanda, and Bree in Roto—,' " I stopped reading and looked to Cameron for help.

"Rotorua," he said. "It's a holiday spot south of here. Bubbling mud pools, geysers, hot springs. It's a fascinating place if you don't mind the smell of sulfur."

I would have asked him how a place that reeked of sulfur had become a vacation destination if he hadn't distracted me by pointing to the last photograph on the mantel shelf.

"Bree again," he said softly.

The last photo—and the only one in color—showed a young teenager standing alone on a beach, with nothing but the sea and sky behind her. Although she was petite, she appeared to be sturdily built. Her heart-shaped face was framed by wind-whipped curtains of lustrous, dark brown hair, and she'd inherited her great-grandfather's beautiful dark eyes. The pretty floral-print summer dress she wore seemed to be at odds with her expression, which was oppressively somber. I found it difficult to connect the grim girl on the beach with the sparkling toddler on the shores of the steaming lake.

"I wonder what happened?" I said again. "Did Ed's drinking drive his wife away? Or did their divorce drive him to drink?"

"Either way, Bree paid the price," said Cameron. "Look at the poor girl's face." He set the photograph down gently. "Let's find her room."

The Pyms' apartment contained two small bedrooms and one large one. One of the small rooms, presumably A. J.'s, was suffused by the musty, medicinal stink of a badly run nursing home. The other, almost certainly Edmund's, was strewn with stubbies and soiled clothes.

The large bedroom had been Bree's.

Bree's room was an island of calm in a sea of chaos. The walls were sky-blue, the furniture was white, and the blue-and-white gingham duvet covering the bed matched the pleated curtains hanging at the window. The gray wall-to-wall carpet was spotless.

The back of the bedroom door was covered by a corkboard, and a computer and printer sat on the clutter-free desk. A set of shelves next to the bed held a collection of small stuffed animals as well as books. A gap in the bottom row of books suggested to me that Bree had brought a favorite volume with her when she'd left home. A small indentation in her pillow made me wonder if she'd taken her favorite stuffed animal—her Reginald—with her as well.

I was reluctant to invade Bree's privacy by going through her things, but Cameron had no such scruples. He systematically searched her dresser, desk, and closet, then knelt to peer under the bed.

"She took the bare essentials," he concluded, getting to his feet. "She must be traveling light. Unusual, for a female."

He gave me a puckish glance and I felt my face turn crimson. The suitcase he'd hauled around for me that morning could not by any stretch of the imagination have been described as light.

Cameron seated himself at the computer, and I left him to it. When it came to the digital age, I was a Neanderthal. I could find my way around a corkboard, however, so while Cameron busied himself at the keyboard, I focused my attention on the drawings, magazine clippings, and photographs Bree had pinned to the back of her door.

Bree Pym was clearly fascinated by the works of J. R. R. Tolkien. Dog-eared copies of his books were on her shelves and she'd plastered her bulletin board with sketches of hobbits, elves, wizards, and strikingly handsome horsemen in leather-clad armor.

"Bree's a big fan of the Lord of the Rings trilogy," I observed.

"No surprise there," Cameron said over his shoulder. "A Kiwi director is making a movie trilogy based on the books. He's filming the entire thing right here in New Zealand. The first part is due out in December, but they're still working on the other two. It's a massive project. Half the country's been involved in it, in one way or another. If Tolkien were alive, we'd make him an honorary citizen."

I turned back to the bulletin board. Cameron's explanation was enlightening, but I wanted to believe that the books had fed Bree's imagination long before the first frames of the films had been shot. A young girl living with an aged grandfather and an alcoholic father might have welcomed an escape into fantasy.

Scattered here and there among the sketches were magazine clippings of romantic cottages surrounded by pretty gardens. It didn't take a degree in psychology to figure out why such images would appeal to a young woman living in squalor.

The photographs pinned to the corkboard were casual shots of teenage boys and girls grinning happily or making goofy faces at the camera. The horrible Jessie had commented caustically about her lodgers' lack of friends, but I wanted to believe that Bree had simply been too embarrassed by the state of her apartment to invite her friends to visit her at home. A girl in her situation needed friends.

A solitary blank spot on the corkboard intrigued me. It measured about six inches by eight inches and had four evenly spaced pins. I wondered what the pins had held, and if Bree had thought it important enough to bring along with her, or if she'd simply thrown it away.

"I know why they stayed in Takapuna," Cameron announced.

"Why?" I asked, turning to face him.

"Bree went to Takapuna Grammar School," he said. "It's an excellent school. Her father—or her grandfather—must have wanted her to have a good education and she didn't disappoint them. She kept an online file of her test scores and they're quite impressive. I also know how the family managed to pay the rent as well as her school fees." He tapped a key and a spreadsheet popped up on the screen. "Bree was the family accountant. She recorded every penny that came in and went out. They survived on A. J.'s old-age pension and the income Bree received from some sort of trust fund. Ed's contributions are erratic at best."

"The landlady told us that he sponged off of his father," I said. "She must have been telling the truth."

"Jessie may be a heartless cow, but I would *never* call her a liar," Cameron said sardonically. "Oh, and there's one more thing," he added nonchalantly. "I know where Bree went."

"Why didn't you say so?" I pelted across the room to peer over his shoulder at the computer screen.

"It's a job application for a waitress position at the Copthorne Hotel and Resort in the Hokianga," he explained. "I found correspondence with the general manager as well. Bree got the job and agreed to show up for work six weeks ago."

"She must have been pretty miserable, to leave home for a waitressing job," I observed.

"There's a phone number," said Cameron. "Shall we call her?"

I pondered for a moment, then shook my head.

"She doesn't know who we are or why we're looking for her," I said. "If we call her, we might scare her off. Let's just go to the hotel."

"My thoughts exactly." Cameron tapped a few keys and the printer began to hum.

"What are you doing?" I said.

"I'm making a copy of Bree's most recent school photograph," he said. "It may come in handy."

As I watched, Bree's heart-shaped face appeared on a hitherto blank piece of paper. She was dressed in what appeared to be a school uniform—pin-striped blazer, light blue shirt, dark blue tie. Her lustrous hair was pulled back from her face with a pale blue ribbon, and her beautiful eyes were as solemn as an undertaker's.

Cameron turned off the computer, collected the copy of Bree's photo from the printer, and got to his feet.

"Where is the Hokianga?" I asked.

"Up north," he informed me.

I thanked him silently for not blinding me with geography, then inquired, "How long will it take us to get there?"

"We can be there by this evening," he said.

I nodded. "How will we get there? Drive?"

"Leave it to me." He glanced at his watch. "I have to make some arrangements before we leave. Will you be all right on your own at the Spencer for a few hours? I'll drop you off now and meet you in the lobby at"—he checked his watch again—"four."

"I'll take a taxi back to the hotel," I said. "I've decided to stay here for a while."

"Suit yourself." Cameron pulled the brass key from his pocket and handed it to me. "If you don't mind my asking, why would you want to stay in this godforsaken place when you could be soaking in the hotel spa?"

"I saw a box of trash bags in the kitchen," I told him. "It's time someone used them. If Bree decides to come home, I don't want her to break an ankle, tripping over her father's empties."

Cameron's smile was so sudden and so sweet that it took my breath away.

"You're a good soul, Lori Shepherd," he said quietly.

"I'm not," I countered, blushing. "I'm just channeling Ruth and Louise."

Nine

I retrieved the biscuit tin from Cameron's rental car before he left, and nibbled on cookies while I waged war on the mess in the apartment. Anzac biscuits, it turned out, were raisinless oatmeal cookies with a pleasing hint of honey and a sturdy texture that kept crumbs to a minimum.

Since the Pyms didn't own a washer or a drier, and since I didn't know where to find a Laundromat, I couldn't do a thing about the unwashed clothes strewn around Ed's bedroom except to confine them to a trash bag, which I placed discretely in his closet. I filled the rest of the bags with fast food wrappers, pizza boxes, beer bottles, and the refrigerator's moldy contents, hauled them to garbage cans behind the house, then got to work on some serious housekeeping.

By the time my taxi arrived, the Pyms' apartment was as clean as I could make it. Although I'd had Bree Pym in mind while I'd vacuumed, dusted, and scrubbed, I'd had her great-grandaunts in my heart. I wouldn't have been able to face Ruth and Louise again if I'd left the place as I'd found it.

Instead of going directly to the Spencer, I asked the cabdriver to drop me off in Takapuna's shopping district. I had lunch at Aubergine, a charming restaurant the cabbie recommended, and withdrew eight hundred dollars in cash from a handy ATM before setting out to make a few necessary purchases. The friendly owner of The Booklover bookstore supplied me with a New Zealand guidebook, which I intended to memorize, as well as directions to a store called Kathmandu, where I bought a day pack and a modest duffel bag.

I was determined to prove to Cameron that Bree Pym wasn't the only female who could travel lightly. I'd been in such a hurry to pack for my unexpected journey that I'd tossed clothes into my suitcase willy-nilly. Now I would take the time to pack intelligently.

When I returned to my suite at the Spencer, I tucked Reginald, the cookie tin, and my brand-new guidebook into the day pack's main compartment and emptied my shoulder bag into its many smaller pockets. I then pared my wardrobe down to seven basic pieces that would see me through a range of temperatures and a variety of social situations. Those pieces fit comfortably in the duffel bag, with room to spare for toiletries, unmentionables, a nightgown, and a pair of black sling-backs that would serve as a dressy alternative to my sneakers. I'd depend on my trusty rain jacket to protect me from New Zealand's changeable spring weather.

I left the rest of my belongings in the large suitcase and delivered it, my shoulder bag, and my carry-on bag to the hotel's checked-luggage room, saying that I would pick them up in a few days.

I returned to my suite with a profound sense of accomplishment and a bone-deep craving for sleep. The jet lag that had left me alone for most of the day had returned with a vengeance. Unfortunately, I couldn't close my eyes until I'd spoken with my nearest and dearest.

I called Bill, to bring him up to speed on my revised itinerary, to find out how the boys' day had gone, and to get an update on Ruth and Louise, who were still alive, if not completely well. Then I settled onto the sofa, opened the blue journal, and tried not to sound as drowsy as I felt.

"Dimity?" I said. "I'm back from Aubrey Pym, Junior's apartment. Things didn't exactly go as planned."

They seldom do, my dear. What happened?

I described our encounters with Jessie the landlady and Bridgette the critical care nurse, and summarized what Cameron and I had learned about A. J., Edmund, and Bree Pym.

Oh, dear. Ruth and Louise will be devastated when they learn that they missed contacting their long-lost nephew by a matter of weeks.

"In Ed's case, it was a matter of hours," I reminded her. "If I'd come one day sooner . . ." I finished the thought with a deep sigh.

If you'd come ten years ago, everything would have been different. Dwelling on "ifs" is pointless, my dear. You came as swiftly as you could.

"True," I said. "And you have to admit that A. J. and Edmund didn't live up to the Pym sisters' standards, in terms of life expectancy. A. J. was only in his late eighties when he died, and Edmund didn't make it to fifty. It's hard to believe they were related to Ruth and Louise."

Environment can trump genetics, Lori. Excessive drinking doesn't usually promote longevity, and no one can help catching pneumonia. Ruth and Louise have been blessed throughout their lives with an abundance of good health and an absence of bad habits. I hope their great-grandniece takes after them. Will you and Cameron Mackenzie attempt to locate her?

"We'll leave for the Hokianga as soon as Cameron gets back to the hotel," I informed her.

Ah, the Hokianga, discovered in the tenth century by Kupe, the great Polynesian explorer. Kupe is considered by some to be the first man to set foot in New Zealand.

I instantly vowed to study my new guidebook assiduously before I spoke with Aunt Dimity again, then asked, "How in heaven's name do you know about the Hokianga?"

One of the soldiers I met in London was from Omapere, a small town in the Hokianga. He described it as a quiet backwater surrounded by great natural beauty. To tell you the truth, he made it sound a bit like Finch.

"Why would an eighteen-year-old girl with a good education take a waitressing job in a quiet backwater?" I asked. "Do you think Bree went there because she needed to put some distance between herself and her father?"

I would read rather more into her actions than a desire to separate herself from her father, Lori. Consider, if you will, the timing of her departure. After heaven knows how many years of looking after her father and her grandfather, her grandfather dies and her father goes on a self-destructive drinking spree. Perhaps Bree couldn't stand it any longer. Perhaps she needed to find someone who would take care of her for a change. Bree may not be running away from someone, Lori. She may be running toward someone.

"A boyfriend?" I guessed.

I doubt that a girl raised in Takapuna would have a boyfriend in the Hokianga. I'm thinking of someone else, someone she lost many years ago.

I frowned down at the journal until an unlikely answer popped into my weary mind.

"Are you talking about her *mother*?" I said skeptically. "I don't think Bree knows where her mother is, Dimity. Ed told Nurse Bridgette that he lost track of his ex-wife after the divorce."

Husbands may lose track of wives, my dear, but children can be extraordinarily persistent when it comes to finding a parent. Bree is an intelligent girl and she had a computer at her disposal. I doubt that she'd have much trouble discovering her mother's current whereabouts.

"You may be right," I said, yawning. Dimity hadn't convinced me, but I was too tired to argue with her. "I guess we'll find out when we get there."

I'm so pleased that we're going to the Hokianga. While we're there you must—you simply MUST—pay your respects to the Lord of the Forest.

"Is he related to the Lord of the Rings?" I asked.

Certainly not. The Lord of the Forest is quite real, Lori, and far older than any character created by Professor Tolkien. Cameron Mackenzie will be able to take you to him. I suggest that you refresh yourself with a short nap. You'll want to be wide-awake during your journey. The scenery will be splendid.

"Talk to you later." I waited until Aunt Dimity's words had faded from the page, then closed the journal, rested my head against the back of the sofa, and let jet lag have its way with me.

Cameron met me in the lobby at four o'clock, as planned. Though he said nothing about my reduced baggage, his smirk spoke volumes. He had, of course, managed to pack everything he needed into a duffel bag smaller than the one I'd bought at Kathmandu.

"Here," I said, handing him the cash I'd withdrawn from the ATM. "I can't let you pay the Pyms' rent. Ruth and Louise wouldn't approve of you throwing your hard-earned money at their problem."

"If you insist, he said.

"I do," I said firmly, and led the way to the car.

After we left the Spencer, I expected to head north, but Cameron confounded me by heading south instead.

"Where are we going?" I asked.

"Back to the airport," he replied.

"Are we flying to the Hokianga?" I asked.

"We'll fly to Dargaville and drive north from there," he answered.

"Excellent," I said, foolishly anticipating a quick and easy journey.

When we reached the Auckland Airport, Cameron bypassed

the international and domestic terminals and parked in a lot reserved for private pilots. Ten minutes later, I found myself strapped into the copilot's seat of a tiny propellor plane, wearing a headset and a worried expression.

"Do you know how to fly this thing?" I said into the little microphone that curved from the headphones to my lips.

Cameron's confident voice came crackling through the headset: "No, but I'm a fast learner." As I started to sputter, he held up a pacifying hand. "Relax, Lori. I've been flying since I was sixteen."

I glanced anxiously at the sky. It looked to me as though New Zealand was about to demonstrate how changeable its spring weather could be.

"Have you noticed the black clouds building up in the west?" I asked.

"A snarky low's coming in off the Tassie," he replied incomprehensibly. Sensing my bewilderment, he said slowly and distinctly, "A low front is moving in from the Tasman Sea. Should make for a lively flight. We have clearance from the tower. Here we go!"

I was glad that I'd taken a nap before leaving the hotel because I couldn't have slept during the journey if I'd been drugged. Gusting winds from the "snarky low" buffeted our tiny plane like a cat toying with a Ping-Pong ball, and sheets of rain obliterated the view. I'd never been airsick in my entire life, but by the time we reached Dargaville, I was cursing the impulse that had prompted me to eat lunch.

Cameron tried to lift my spirits by telling me that we would land on the Dargaville Aerodrome's limestone runway rather than its grass strip, but the news that we would be landing at an airport that still *had* a grass strip failed signally to boost my morale. I gripped the edge of my seat and apologized mutely for every sin

I'd ever committed as he zeroed in on the rain-washed runway, but after a few heart-stopping bounces, we were safely on the ground and taxiing toward a small hangar.

My hands shook as I removed the headset and it took me three tries to undo the restraining straps, but I managed to keep my trembling knees from buckling when my feet finally hit solid ground. I pulled up the hood on my rain jacket and let Cameron retrieve all of the luggage. I felt he deserved to be punished for predicting that the flight from hell would be "lively."

"Camo! Over here, bro!" called a voice.

A stocky man with light brown skin waved to us from the shelter of the hangar. He was dressed in a knee-length slicker, shorts, and flip-flops, and his coal-black hair was clipped close to his skull. Around his neck dangled a curiously carved pendant of highly polished, dark green stone, and his bare legs were covered from ankle to thigh with an elegant, curving pattern of intertwined tattoos.

"Toko!" called Cameron. "Good to see you, man!"

During the introductions that followed, I learned that Toko Baker was a Maori—the first I'd met—and one of Cameron's oldest friends. The two men chatted briefly in Toko's native tongue before reverting to English.

"Flight all right?" Toko asked me, winking at Cameron.

"Piece of cake," I lied, with a carefree shrug.

"Jean Batten would be proud of you, Lori." Cameron dropped his bag and clapped me on the back. "She was New Zealand's Amelia Earhart, and as fearless as they come, but compared to you, she was a quaking blancmange."

"Thanks, Camo," I said through gritted teeth.

"Car's waiting for you outside," said Toko. "I'll look after the kite."

"Ta, Toko," said Cameron.

"Hei aha," Toko replied, adding for my benefit, "No worries, mate."

"We're borrowing one of Toko's vehicles," Cameron said as his friend headed for the plane. "He takes a laissez-faire approach to maintenance, so we won't be breaking any land-speed records, but we'll get where we need to go. Only sixty-three kilometers left— round about forty miles."

"Why didn't we fly to an airport closer to the hotel?" I asked.

"There isn't one," he replied. "And I didn't think you'd enjoy a paddock landing."

I didn't know what a paddock landing was, but if it was more lively than the landing we'd just made, I was quite sure that I would have hated it.

It rained so hard for the next sixty-three kilometers that we might as well have driven through a tunnel. The scenery Aunt Dimity had praised so highly flashed past in a misty blur. The two-lane road was narrow, hilly, winding, and punctuated by a series of orange signs that featured nothing but a black exclamation point. I soon learned that the exclamation point was a general warning to slow down for a variety of reasons, ranging from road repairs to minor landslides to gaping craters in the middle of our lane. Thankfully, there was little traffic, and Toko's car was so grossly underpowered that we didn't really need to slow down to avoid anything.

Cameron insisted that we make one stop along the way, in a place called Waipoua Forest. I began to suspect that Aunt Dimity had somehow influenced his decision when a five-minute hike along a boardwalk snaking through a sodden jungle took us to the base of a gigantic tree known as Tane Mahuta, or the Lord of the Forest.

The tree's massive trunk soared upward to a crown of stumpy branches covered with mosses, ferns, and vines, as though it were presenting its own miniature rain forest to the sky. Tane Mahuta's girth, Cameron proclaimed, was just over forty-five feet, and it was nearly 170 feet tall.

"It's a kauri," he said proudly. "One hundred percent native to New Zealand. The logging industry took a bite out of our kauri forests in the late 1800s, but Tane Mahuta and some of his cousins were spared. They're the oldest living things in the Southern Hemisphere." Rain pelted his face as he tilted his head back to savor the tree's magnificence. "I know you're pressed for time, Lori, but we couldn't pass by without saying hello."

I didn't debate the point. I felt such reverence for the ancient tree that I forgot about the rotten weather, the terrifying flight, and the hazardous drive, and wanted only to linger awhile in Tane Mahuta's majestic presence. When Cameron mentioned that it would soon be dark, however, I came to my senses and galloped back to the car. Nothing short of a medical emergency could have induced me to travel on that road at night.

Darkness had fallen by the time we reached the Copthorne Hotel and Resort. The graveled parking lot was dimly lit, but the hotel appeared to be a sprawling British Colonial house to which a modern, two-story wing had been added. Palm trees, ferns, and tropical flowers grew in small beds on either side of the entrance, and the muted boom of the surf suggested that we weren't too far from the sea.

The modest lobby was paneled in dark wood and decorated with Maori artifacts. A printed sign on one wall told the story of Kupe, the great Polynesian navigator. I had time to read most of it, because Ms. Campbell, the middle-aged receptionist, had to finish what sounded like a complicated phone call before she could attend to us.

After verifying the reservations Cameron had made, Ms. Campbell told us that the hotel's restaurant was still serving dinner and that we would be in the first and second rooms on the upper floor of the modern wing.

"There's no direct connection between the buildings, I'm afraid," she said apologetically. "You'll have to go outside again to reach your rooms. It's only a few steps away, though, and I think the rain's let up a bit. Will you be dining with us this evening?"

"Yes," Cameron and I chorused.

The receptionist smiled. "I'll reserve a table for you. Come down when you're ready." She gestured to a hallway that led off of the lobby. "The dining room is through there."

"Is Bree Pym on the dinner shift?" I asked hopefully.

Ms. Campbell's warm smile wilted and her gaze became guarded. "Miss Bree Pym is no longer employed by the Copthorne."

"She's not?" I said, blinking in disbelief. "But we've come so far. . . ." My words trailed off into a faintly pathetic whine.

"Are you family?" Ms. Campbell inquired.

"No," I said. "I'm trying to contact Bree Pym on behalf of her relatives in England. I have important information to give her. My friend and I have gone to a great deal of trouble to come here tonight because we expected to find her working at your hotel."

"I'm sorry to hear that she's inconvenienced you," Ms. Campbell said, "but I can't say that I'm surprised." Her voice rose in righteous indignation. "She left us without a word of warning after only four days on the job. I *still* haven't found a replacement. Far be it from me to speak ill of anyone, but I'm forced to say that I found Miss Pym to be thoughtless, irresponsible, and unreliable."

"One moment," said Cameron. He reached into an inner pocket of his rain jacket and pulled out the picture he'd printed in Bree's bedroom. He unfolded it and held it out to the receptionist, asking, "Is this the girl you hired?"

"That's Bree," she said curtly. "I never forget a face, especially a face I never want to see again."

"Thank you," said Cameron, returning the photo to his pocket. "We'll go to our rooms now."

Since there was no bellhop service, Cameron and I carried our bags through the rain, which was falling as heavily as ever, and up an outdoor flight of steps to an exterior walkway. Guest rooms lined one side of the walkway. The other side overlooked the parking area.

"A shame about the weather." Cameron paused at the walkway's railing and peered upward. "If the sky would clear, I could show you the Southern Cross. It's not the biggest or the brightest constellation, but it was so useful to early explorers that we put it on our flag."

"I don't think we'll do much stargazing tonight," I grumbled. Our failure to find Bree had soured my mood, as had the unrelenting downpour. Though I was yearning to put a solid roof over my head, I crossed to stand beside Cameron. "Do you find it hard to believe? About Bree, I mean."

"We'll talk during dinner," he replied. "Can you be ready in thirty minutes?"

"Make it twenty," I said.

My room was simply but adequately furnished. The wall opposite the door was made entirely of glass, with a sliding glass door that gave access to a small balcony. Since I had no desire to step outside any sooner than I had to, I ignored the balcony, changed into a silk blouse, black trousers, and the sling-backs, and placed my wet jeans and sneakers near the room's heater, hoping against hope that they would dry before morning. I didn't relish the thought of traveling back to Auckland in squelchy sneakers.

I opened the door at Cameron's first knock.

"You're dressed," he said, looking surprised. "I thought my wife was the only woman on earth who could change for dinner in less than thirty minutes."

"I'm full of surprises, Camo," I said, zipping my rain jacket.

"Are you going to call me Camo from now on?" he asked as we retraced our steps to the lobby.

"If you're lucky," I shot back.

A young, heavyset waitress dressed all in black met us at the dining room entrance and guided us to a table near a huge picture window through which we could see nothing but gloom. The dining room seemed extracavernous because only two other tables were taken.

"It's off season," Cameron explained.

"I'll say," I muttered.

I was too disheartened to take much interest in food, so Cameron ordered the freshly caught crayfish and a bottle of locally produced chardonnay for both of us. When the waitress departed, I gazed at the rain-streaked window and shook my head.

"I can't believe that the girl described by the receptionist is the same girl who lived in Takapuna," I said. "Bree was a top student. She was the family's accountant. Her room was as neat as a pin. How could she suddenly turn into an irresponsible slacker?"

"Maybe she's taking some time off," Cameron suggested.

"Excuse me." Our waitress had returned, carrying an ice bucket and the bottle of wine Cameron had ordered. She glanced over her shoulder, then continued in a low voice, "What do you want with Bree? She's not in trouble, is she?"

"Not with us," said Cameron. "We're friends of the family."

"We're not upset with her," I added. "We're worried about her."

The waitress opened the bottle, poured wine into Cameron's glass, and waited until he'd nodded his approval before filling my glass. As she slid the bottle into the ice bucket, she seemed to reach a decision.

"You shouldn't believe everything Ms. Campbell tells you," she said abruptly.

"What should we believe, Miss . . . ?" Cameron raised an eyebrow.

"Call me Alison," said the waitress. She glanced over her shoulder again before adding in an urgent undertone, "What happened was, he broke her heart. That's why she left."

"Who broke whose heart?" I asked in some confusion.

"Daniel broke Bree's heart," said Alison. "He didn't mean to, but he did."

"Who is Daniel?" asked Cameron.

"Daniel Rivers," Alison replied. "He's an artist. He lives south of here. Every once in a while a girl lands on his doorstep, hoping to shack up with him."

"Is that why Bree came here?" I asked.

Alison nodded. "I told her she had as much chance of bonking Daniel as I have of becoming prime minister. Daniel may be an artist, but he's also a very happily married man."

"Which is why he sent her away," said Cameron.

"He tried to let her down easy," Alison explained. "He had a long heart-to-heart with her, but it didn't help. She came back from his place in tears. Packed her bag and left the next day."

"Do you know where she went?" I asked.

"Sorry." Alison shook her head. "Daniel might, though. Lord knows what Bree told him."

"Can you give us his phone number?" Cameron asked.

"Sorry," Alison repeated with an apologetic shrug.

"Can you tell us where he lives?" I asked.

"I'll do better than that," said Alison. "I'll draw you a map. You'll need one. Daniel lives in the wop-wops." Her brow wrinkled. "Bree was in tatters when she took off. Someone needs to find that girl before she does something stupid. I'll be back in two ticks with your crayfish."

She returned a few minutes later with a roughly drawn map and the biggest crayfish I'd ever seen. She handed the map to Cameron before placing several dishes before us.

"When you find Bree, tell her I'm thinking of her." Alison smiled sadly, then hastened to wait on another table.

After studying the map, Cameron proposed a plan of action. "We'll check out of the hotel tomorrow morning and drive straight to Daniel Rivers's place. If he can't tell us where Bree went, we'll have no choice but to return to Auckland."

"Okay," I said absently. I couldn't take my eyes off the humongous crustacean spilling over the edges of my plate. "Are you sure this is a crayfish? It looks like a lobster."

"You're accustomed to freshwater crayfish," Cameron said wisely. "These beauties come from the sea. After you've had your first mouthful, you'll wish they were bigger. They're succulent, sweet, and altogether delicious."

Renewed hope had restored my appetite, but before attacking my meal, I raised my glass of chardonnay and proposed a toast.

"To saltwater crayfish," I said. "And to a fresh lead."

Cameron waved Alison's map in triumph as he touched his glass to mine.

Ten

My first task upon returning to my room after dinner was to telephone Bill. He informed me that all was well on the home front, that Ruth and Louise were delighted to know that they had a great-grandniece, and that they approved of my decision to deliver their letter to her. I explained yet again why I wouldn't be on the first available flight back to England.

"Don't worry about it," he urged. "Just find the girl."

"I'm trying," I assured him, "but she's not cooperating."

Bill called Will and Rob to the phone, and after they demonstrated that they knew more about New Zealand than Mummy did—"No, Mummy, kangaroos live in *Australia*"—I said good night, plugged the cell phone in to recharge, and packed my "nice" clothes in the duffel bag to get a head start on the morning.

I climbed into bed at nine o'clock, warmed to my toes by a hot bath and filled to the bursting point with sweet, succulent, and altogether delicious crayfish. Though drowsy, I opened the blue journal and brought Aunt Dimity up to speed on my action-packed day.

She was sorry that the weather had prevented me from enjoying the scenery, pleased that I'd met the Lord of the Forest, and gracious in defeat when she learned that Bree hadn't come north to find her mother but to seduce a married man.

"I think Bree must be having some sort of breakdown," I said. "She certainly doesn't sound like the girl with the dog-eared books, the cute stuffed animals, and the blue gingham duvet."

Bree has been holding her family together with both hands, Lori. Girls burdened with too much responsibility sometimes find it necessary to rebel.

"They do," I said, nodding.

It's possible, of course, that Alison misunderstood Bree's intentions. Do you remember the sketches you found pinned to the bulletin board in Bree's bedroom? You told me that they were quite good. Perhaps she approached Mr. Rivers for advice on artistic endeavors.

"She just wanted to show him her sketches?" I said with a juicy chuckle.

I suspect that fatigue has made you giddy, Lori.

"I'd blame it on the local chardonnay," I interjected happily. "It's superb."

I'll leave you to sleep it off, shall I? We can continue our discussion after you've spoken with Mr. Rivers.

"Good night, Dimity," I murmured.

Sleep well, my dear, though I doubt that you'll need my encouragement. Your first day in New Zealand has been nothing if not eventful.

I closed the journal and placed it beside Reginald, who sat beneath the lamp on the bedside table.

"Dimity likes to think well of people, and I love her for it," I said to my pink bunny. "But sometimes she misses the obvious. It's pretty clear to me that Bree came here to pounce on Daniel Rivers. I just hope he knows where she went. The Pyms can't hold on forever, and I can't spend the rest of my life chasing after a confused teenager."

I touched a finger to Reg's snout, turned out the light, and surrendered myself to the soft pillows and the sound of the booming surf.

* * *

Since I'd forgotten to close the glass wall's shutters before drifting off to sleep, I awoke to a sun-drenched room and a view that made my jaw drop as I sat up in bed. A moment later I was on the balcony, drinking in scenery that fulfilled every promise Aunt Dimity had made.

An intensely blue, sparkling bay lay before me, embraced by a broad expanse of golden dunes to the north and a lush green headland to the south. An emerald lawn ran down from the hotel to a flawless crescent of tawny sand at the water's edge. A flock of gulls soared above waves frilled by an onshore breeze, and a host of tiny birds twittered in the branches of a solitary pohutukawa tree that grew not ten yards from where I stood. There wasn't a cloud in the sky.

I was faintly puzzled by the presence of a small swimming pool in the deck area adjacent to the hotel's main building. The pristine beach made a swimming pool seem redundant.

"The bay is called Hokianga Harbor," said Cameron, poking his head around the wall that divided my balcony from his. "Not bad, eh?"

"Not bad at all," I agreed. "How did you know I was out here?"

"I heard your glass door open," he said. "I've been up for an hour."

"Bully for you." I wrinkled my nose at him, then nodded toward the deck area. "Why the pool? If I'd brought a bathing suit with me, I'd swim in the bay."

"Not for long," he said, with a wry smile. "Hokianga Harbor is a breeding ground for great white sharks."

"Yikes," I said, eyeing the sparkling waters with new respect. "It sure is pretty, though."

"Yes, it is," said Cameron. "Ready for breakfast?"

"Believe it or not, I am," I told him. "See you in twenty."

I paused for one last look at the dunes, the headland, and the shining bay, then raced inside to splash water on my face, slip into a T-shirt, jeans, and sneakers, and finish packing. I didn't want to spoil my reputation as a twenty-minute wonder.

After plundering the hotel's breakfast buffet and saying a final good-bye to Alison, we checked out of the hotel, climbed into Toko's car, and drove south along State Highway 12, retracing the route we'd taken north the previous evening. While I craned my neck to take in the intensely green hills, the stunning seascapes, and the quirky holiday houses that had hitherto been obscured by rain, Cameron paid attention to Alison's map.

We left the highway at the impossibly named village of Waiotemarama and turned onto a dirt road that felt as though it had last been graded in the early 1950s. Toko's car developed an alarming number of new rattles as we juddered across the road's washboard surface and zigzagged gingerly around its rain-filled potholes.

The dirt road took us into a kauri forest so dense that the canopy dimmed the bright sunlight. As we inched along, I heard bird calls I'd never heard before and saw flowers that would have been the pride of any greenhouse in England growing wild and in astonishing profusion. Finally, Cameron pulled off of the road and parked in the grassy, uphill driveway of a five-sided house on stilts.

The house's roof was made of corrugated iron and its outer walls were covered in orange shingles. Three peacocks—one male and two females—perched on the wooden railing of its elevated front porch, and the clearing in which it stood looked as though it had been shorn by a flock of sheep. A tree dripping with bright yellow blossoms stood in the center of an octagonal picnic table that occupied the only piece of level ground I'd seen since we'd left the hotel.

"Looks like an artist's house to me," I commented.

"Very atmospheric," Cameron agreed.

"And the guy with the paintbrush is a dead giveaway," I concluded.

A man holding a slender paintbrush stood hunched over the picnic table. He was several inches shorter than Cameron and more slightly built. His features were pleasant, but not particularly memorable, and his short-cropped brown hair was touched with gray at the temples. He was dressed in a baggy gray sweater, faded jeans, and black flip-flops.

"I'd like to have the flip-flop concession in this country," I murmured.

"We call them jandals," Cameron murmured back. "It's short for Japanese sandals. They're a popular form of footwear in New Zealand."

"I've noticed," I said dryly.

We got out of the car. The paraphernalia on the picnic table suggested that the man was working on a watercolor. I was sorry to interrupt his creative flow, but he didn't seem to mind. He dropped his brush into a water-filled jam jar and smiled amiably as we approached.

"Lost?" he asked.

"Not if you're Daniel Rivers," said Cameron.

"I am," said the man, folding his arms. "So you must be in the right place. What can I do for you?"

"My name is Cameron Mackenzie," said Cameron, "and this is my friend Lori Shepherd. We're looking for a young woman. Her name is Aubrey Aroha Pym."

Daniel's smile faded and he glanced anxiously toward the house. "May I ask why you're looking for her?"

"I've come all the way from England to deliver an important message to her on behalf of some distant relatives," I explained. "Alison at the Copthorne told us that you might know where she is."

"You'd better speak with my wife." Daniel gestured toward the benches surrounding the octagonal table. "Have a seat. I'll get her."

Cameron and I chose a bench on the far side of the table, where we had an unimpeded view of the house. Daniel crossed the clearing, climbed the stairs, and went through the front door. Several minutes passed before the door opened again. When it did, I stiffened slightly and gasped in surprise.

The woman who followed Daniel onto the elevated porch was in every respect save one the spitting image of Bree Pym. She had the same petite build, the same heart-shaped face, and the same long, lustrous dark hair, but her eyes were sea green instead of rich brown.

"She was right," I said under my breath. "Bree *was* looking for her mother."

Cameron gave me a questioning look. "She?"

"Never mind," I muttered. Nothing on God's green earth could have forced me to admit to Cameron Mackenzie that I had an invisible friend who wrote to me on the pages of a blank journal.

The woman was barefoot and the hem of her colorful cotton dress brushed the grass as she walked toward us. Her sole piece of jewelry was a polished stone pendant similar to the one Toko Baker had worn. She carried herself with great dignity, but her expression was difficult to read.

Cameron and I stood as her husband presented her to us.

"Amanda Rivers," he said. "My wife."

"I think our guests would like a cold drink, Daniel," said Amanda.

When her husband hesitated, she reached out to squeeze his hand, as if to tell him that she would be all right without him. He kissed her forehead and went back into the house.

Amanda motioned for us to be seated and lowered herself gracefully onto the bench opposite ours. She studied us in silence, then asked abruptly, "Did Ed send you?"

My heart plummeted. In the rush of events, I'd forgotten that Nurse Bridgette had been unable to communicate with Edmund Pym's ex-wife, either before or after his death. I didn't want to be the bearer of such tragic tidings, but I couldn't think of any way around it.

"No," I replied. "Ed didn't send us. I came to New Zealand on behalf of two Englishwomen named Ruth and Louise Pym. Ruth and Louise are Bree's great-grandaunts."

"They're real," Amanda said half to herself.

"I beg your pardon?" I said.

"I thought the English aunts were a fantasy," she told me. "Ed cursed them sometimes, when he was drunk. I thought he invented them."

"He didn't," I said. "Ruth and Louise Pym are as real as you and me." I clasped my hands together and leaned forward on the picnic table. "I shouldn't be the one telling you this, Amanda, but there's something you need to know." I took a steadying breath and looked her straight in the eyes. "Edmund Pym passed away yesterday morning."

Her expression remained impassive as she asked, "Was he alone?"

"No," I said. "He was in the hospital. A nurse was with him when he died."

"He drank himself to death?" she asked.

I nodded.

"Bree thought he would," she said. "She told me he went on a bender after A. J. died. She took off because she couldn't bear to watch her father kill himself." Amanda lowered her eyes. "I didn't leave her with *him,* you know. I left her with her grandparents. They disowned Ed years before he met me, but they welcomed their granddaughter with open arms." She shook her head. "I thought Bree would be safe with them. I never dreamed that they would take Ed back."

I glanced uncertainly at Cameron. Amanda's confession had caught me off guard. The news of Ed's death had evidently reawakened memories she'd tried to forget.

"Amanda," I said, "you don't have to explain yourself to us."

"I'm not," she said softly. "I'm trying to remember why I abandoned my child."

"I'm sure you wanted what was best for her," said Cameron.

"I did," said Amanda, still gazing at the table. "Ed didn't just drink, you know. He gambled, lied, slept around. I waited far too long to divorce him. By the time we split, I was a broken woman. I was certainly an unfit mother." Amanda closed her eyes and sighed heavily. "Bree's grandparents made me promise not to contact her after they took her in. I was willing to make the sacrifice because I believed they would raise her properly, send her to a good school, see to it that she had everything I couldn't give her. I didn't know that Ed would worm his way back into their good graces."

"Bree went to a fine school," Cameron offered. "She was an excellent student."

"School was her only escape from the hell Ed created at home." Amanda clenched her jaw. "If I'd known what was happening . . . But I never dreamed . . ." Her words trailed off.

"I thought she was a tramper," said Daniel.

I looked up, startled. I'd been so absorbed in Amanda's story that I hadn't noticed Daniel's return. He carried a wooden tray laden with four tall glasses and a glass pitcher filled with freshly made lemonade.

"There's a bush walk not far from here," he said, placing the tray on the table. "It leads to a waterfall. When Bree turned into our drive, I thought she was a tramper looking for the waterfall."

"But she was a daughter, looking for her mother," Amanda murmured.

Daniel sat beside his wife and put an arm around her.

"How did she find you?" Cameron asked.

"She read an article about me in an art magazine," Daniel replied. He looked at the yellow blossoms dangling overhead. "The article featured a photograph of me and Amanda, sitting here, beneath the kowhai."

"Bree recognized me straightaway," said Amanda. "She's a bright girl. It didn't take her long to track me down."

"If she knew where to find you," I said, "why did she take the job at the Copthorne?"

"She didn't want me to think that she'd come here, wanting a handout," said Amanda. "She wanted to prove to me that she wasn't like her father." Sunlight rippled on her dark hair as she shook her head. "As if I needed proof. . . ."

Daniel filled the glasses and passed them around, but no one drank.

"It took my wife a long time to recover from her marriage to

Ed," he said. "When I met her, she was ready to begin a new life. We married and started a family of our own."

"We have two boys and a girl," said Amanda. "They're at school now, but they were at home when Bree turned up."

"We asked her to stay, to become a part of our family," said Daniel, "but she didn't want to intrude."

"I think she was crushed when she saw our children," said Amanda, "especially our daughter. Bree must have felt as if I'd replaced her. I'm sure it's why she quit her job at the Copthorne. She couldn't stand to be near me. She felt as though I'd abandoned her all over again." Amanda swallowed hard, but her gaze was steady when her eyes met mine. "What do her English aunts want with her?"

"I don't know for certain," I admitted. "The letter they asked me to deliver was originally meant for A. J., but I arrived too late to give it to him or to his son. Since Bree is A. J.'s granddaughter, they want me to give it to her."

"There's a bit of urgency involved," Cameron chimed in. "Bree's great-grandaunts are quite elderly now, and they're seriously ill. We're racing the clock to find Bree before they run out of time. Do you know where she went after she left the Copthorne?"

"Ohakune," Amanda answered promptly. "She told me that she had a friend there who could find her a job."

"Did she tell you the friend's name?" I asked.

"Angelo. He owns a café, apparently," said Amanda. "I didn't press her for details. At this late date, it would have been presumptuous of me to claim a mother's right to pry into her business."

Cameron turned to Daniel. "How did Bree get here? Does she have a car?"

Daniel nodded. "An aging Ford Laser. Half red paint, half rust."

"It was A. J.'s," Amanda put in. "Bree said it was all he could afford after Ed gambled away his savings at the track."

An uncomfortable silence fell. I had no idea how to conclude such a painful conversation. I wanted to jump into Toko's car and take off for Ohakune immediately but "Thanks a bunch, gotta run" seemed a tad insensitive. I breathed a sigh of relief when Cameron found the right words to say.

"Is there anything you'd like us to tell Bree when we speak with her?" he asked.

"Yes, please," said Amanda. "Tell my daughter that I've held her in my heart from the moment she was born. Tell her no one else can fill that space. Tell her she has always been and will always be my *taonga*."

"My treasure," Cameron murmured to me.

"Tell her . . ." Amanda's voice betrayed not a quiver of emotion, but tears filled her green eyes and spilled down her cheeks as she reached for Daniel's hand. "Tell her that our home will always be hers."

"We'll tell her," Cameron promised.

We exchanged phone numbers with Amanda and Daniel, thanked them for their time, and left them sitting hand in hand beneath the kowhai. We bumped and juddered for a half mile before either one of us spoke.

"No wonder Bree was a mess when she left the Copthorne," I said. "The poor kid had her heart broken, all right, but not by Daniel." I gazed forlornly at a clump of long-stemmed lilies growing along the side of the road. "I understand why she needed to leave the Hokianga, but I wish she hadn't. I don't know how we're going to track her down in Ohakune. Angelo-who-runs-a-café isn't much to go on."

"Ohakune isn't Las Vegas, Lori," said Cameron. "It's a very small town. If Bree's still there, we won't have any trouble finding her."

"If . . . ," I said, sighing.

We lapsed into a thoughtful silence and didn't speak again until we were seated at Morrell's Café in Waimamaku, where we stopped to grab a quick bite of lunch.

"What's the plan?" I asked, after I'd swallowed my first mouthful of a scrumptious vegetarian quiche. "How do we get to Ohakune?"

"We drive to Dargaville and fly south," said Cameron.

I paused with a forkful of quiche halfway to my mouth. "How far south?"

"Far enough," he said.

I lowered my fork and eyed him suspiciously. "Are you telling me . . . ?"

"That's right, Lori," he said cheerfully. "You're about to visit one of New Zealand's most active volcanic regions. Won't it be fun?"

"Oh, joy," I said, pushing my quiche to the side.

It seemed to me that, between snarky lows and active volcanoes, I'd be lucky to survive my trip Down Under.

Eleven

We pulled in to the Dargaville Aerodrome at half past two. While Cameron made a few phone calls, I chatted with Toko Baker, who'd come to collect his car and who cheerfully accepted a handful of Anzac biscuits from Donna's tin. When I offered to pay for any damage the dirt road might have done to his vehicle, Toko responded with a hearty laugh and a carefree wave of his hand.

"It's my boy's car," he said. "It'll do him good to repair it. How else will he learn?"

After tossing our bags into the plane's cargo compartment, Cameron conducted a thorough flight inspection, boosted me into the cockpit, climbed into the pilot's seat, and waved good-bye to his friend. Toko stuck around long enough to watch us take off, then puttered slowly away in his son's underpowered and much abused car.

Thanks to calmer weather, my second flight in New Zealand was less lively than the first and I was able to appreciate the beauty of the landscape unfolding beneath me. The small villages, the farmsteads, and the intensely green, sheep-dotted fields surrounding them reminded me forcibly of the Irish countryside, which came as a bit of a surprise, as I'd spent the morning in a subtropical rain forest.

When a small cluster of snowcapped peaks came into view, I began to understand what Cameron had meant when he'd said that his country was "many things." New Zealand, it seemed, packed a lot of variety into a relatively small number of square kilometers.

The only spine-tingling moment occurred when we swooped in to land on a runway that appeared to end mere inches from the edge of an enormous lake. I held my breath until a few hard bumps on the tarmac assured me that we'd made a touchdown instead of a splashdown.

"Lake Taupo," Cameron informed me, as we taxied to the airport's modest terminal. "The largest lake in New Zealand. Its waters conceal the crater of a volcano that erupted twenty-seven thousand years ago."

"Must have been a big bang," I commented, squinting to make out the lake's distant shores.

"Compared to it, the Mount Saint Helens eruption was a kitten's hiccough," said Cameron.

"How far are we from Ohakune?" I asked.

"About a hundred and twenty kilometers," he replied. "An old friend of mine lives near Taupo."

I cocked my head to one side. "Does your old friend happen to have a car we can borrow?"

"You're catching on," he said, grinning.

Cameron's friend, Aidan Dun, was a professional trout fisherman who made a living by teaching his craft, participating in fly-fishing competitions, and guiding enthusiasts to well-stocked local streams around Lake Taupo. Aidan's car, a hunter green Jeep Cherokee, was in much better shape than the one we'd borrowed from Toko, but its interior had a distinctly fishy aroma.

"I've always wanted to smell like a dead trout," I said, opening my window.

"The angler's perfume," crooned my irrepressible companion.

As we drove south along Lake Taupo's eastern shore, I fixed my gaze on the three snowcapped mountains I'd seen from the plane.

At ground level, they looked like paper cutouts pasted against the clear blue sky. The one in the middle resembled a child's drawing of a volcano—a perfect cone with black slopes and a whipped-cream summit. Happily, it wasn't spewing clouds of ash or dribbling the rivers of molten lava my sons felt compelled to add to every drawing they made of a volcano.

"We're coming up on Tongariro National Park," Cameron announced. "It's the fourth oldest national park in the world, home to Mount Tongariro, Mount Ngauruhoe, and Mount Ruapehu. Tongariro's been asleep for a long time, but Ngauruhoe—the pretty one in the middle—let off some steam in 1975, and Ruapehu belched a few tons of ash in 1996. Do you ski?"

"No," I replied.

"A pity," he said. "Ruapehu has two first-class ski areas."

"Aren't the skiers put off by all the belching?" I asked.

"Our vulcanologists issue warnings and most people pay attention to them," said Cameron. "When the mountain settles down, they hit the slopes again." He gave me a sidelong glance. "Ohakune's at the foot of Mount Ruapehu, Lori. It's a ski town. Its population explodes in winter."

"It sounds as though the population isn't the only thing that explodes," I commented, peering apprehensively through the windshield.

"My point is," Cameron went on, "in July or August, Bree would be lost in a crowd of skiers and snowboarders. Luckily for us, the high season ended in September."

While I tried to wrap my head around the notion of winter in July, my native guide drove on.

*   *   *

I wasn't sure why a ski town would erect a giant carrot at one end of its main thoroughfare until Cameron explained that Ohakune was New Zealand's carrot capital.

"Farming has been around a lot longer than skiing," he observed, "and carrots flourish in Ohakune's volcanic soil. If you're ever here in July, don't miss the Carrot Festival. It's sort of an orange-tinted Mardi—"

"Stop!" I cried.

"—Gras," Cameron finished. He regarded me ruefully. "If you're tired of my travelogue, Lori—"

"I'm not tired of your travelogue," I said impatiently. "I want you to stop the *car*." I jabbed a thumb over my shoulder. "We just passed Angelo's Café!"

Cameron promptly exceeded his instructions by executing a tidy U-turn and pulling into the café's deserted parking lot. He left the engine running while we took stock of the situation.

"No cars in the parking lot," he commented.

"No lights in the windows," I observed.

"And no smoke rising from the chimney." He sighed. "I'm sorry, Lori, but it doesn't look very promising."

Angelo's Café was a modern one-story building with large windows, white clapboard siding, and a peaked roof made of bright blue corrugated iron. A hand-lettered sign hanging inside its glass front door confirmed the conclusion Cameron and I had already reached.

" 'Closed for the season,' " he read aloud.

I eyed the sign resentfully and muttered, "Curses, foiled again."

"Not necessarily," said Cameron. "The café may be closed, but I'm willing to bet that Angelo lives in Ohakune. Bree may be staying with him while she works for someone else." He turned the Jeep around, exited the parking lot, and continued driving past an assortment of motels, small businesses, and private homes. "Who knows? We may find her behind the reception desk at our hotel."

"If not, we can drive up and down the streets of Ohakune, shouting her name," I suggested.

"That's the spirit," Cameron said bracingly.

Cameron had booked us into the Powderhorn Chateau, an upscale hotel with a pleasantly low-key atmosphere. The place had all the hallmarks of a classic Swiss chalet—vine-draped balconies, pine-clad walls, exposed wooden rafters, and uneven floors that gave it a comfortably settled feeling. As we checked in at the front desk, the hotel's resident cat—a plump orange-and-white tabby—watched us from the shelter of a small grotto tucked into a shadowy corner beside the lobby's main entrance.

The slender, blond receptionist was dressed casually in a blue cardigan, a white T-shirt, cropped khaki pants, and blue sneakers. Her name tag identified her as Teresa Walsh. While Cameron and I filled out our registration forms, Teresa nodded at the cat.

"If she follows you to your room," she told us, "feel free to close the door on her."

"If she follows me to my room, Teresa, I'll *open* the door for her," said Cameron, glancing over his shoulder. "I can tell by look-ing at her that she's a sweetheart."

As if on cue, the cat leaped out of the grotto and strode over to entwine herself between Cameron's legs, purring volubly. He squatted down to stroke her, murmuring endearments that would have sent Stanley into raptures.

Teresa touched a finger to her eyeglasses and beamed at him. She seemed to approve of tall, good-looking men who loved cats.

"Teresa," he said, straightening, "would you happen to know if a young woman named Bree Pym works here?"

"Sorry," she said, and she looked genuinely crestfallen. "The name doesn't ring a bell and I know everyone on staff."

"Never mind," Cameron said gently. "I'm sure you know Angelo."

Teresa's face brightened. "Angelo Velesuonno? The Yank who runs the café? *Everyone* knows Angelo."

"He's a great guy, isn't he?" Cameron said smoothly. "I was hoping to say hello to him before I leave town." He rested his elbows on the reception counter, leaned closer to her, and added in a semi-seductive murmur, "The problem is, Teresa, I've lost his address. I know it's asking a lot, and I don't want you to do anything that might compromise the position of trust you hold at the chateau, but I'd be enormously grateful to you, Teresa, if you'd tell me where Angelo lives."

Cameron's tactics were as unsubtle as two buckets of lard, but they worked. Teresa's diminutive bosom heaved each time he said her name. If the humidity had been a bit higher, I think her glasses would have fogged up. It took her a breathless moment to find her voice.

"You don't have to leave the hotel to speak with Angelo," she said. "He and his wife have an eight o'clock dinner reservation at the Matterhorn—the restaurant upstairs. If you like, I can make an eight o'clock reservation for you, too."

Cameron's purr was almost indistinguishable from the cat's.

"Teresa," he said, "you are a peach."

The young woman blushed to her roots as she scribbled our

names in the reservation book, and giggled when she handed us our keys.

"I know a few Ringers who would kill to have your rooms," she informed us.

"Ringers?" I said.

"Lord of the Rings fans," Cameron explained.

"You've heard about the movie trilogy?" Teresa asked.

"Of course," said Cameron. "I can't wait to see it!" His expression radiated interest.

"The principle cast members and the director stayed here while they were filming on Ruapehu," Teresa went on. "Usually their rooms are booked by Ringers, but a few are free tonight." She turned to me. "I've given you Elijah Wood's room. He's Frodo."

"The hobbit? What a treat!" I gushed because she seemed to expect it of me.

"I've put *you* in Sir Ian McKellen's room," she said, favoring Cameron with a brilliant smile. "He's Gandalf."

"The wizard." Cameron bowed. "I'm honored, Teresa. And thank you—thank you for *everything*."

She blushed again and ducked her head so rapidly that her glasses slid to the tip of her nose. She pushed them up and gazed at Cameron with undisguised admiration until we boarded the elevator. The cat came with us.

"What a performance," I said, after the door slid shut. "You'd think she'd be used to actors by now, but she fell for your act, hook, line, and sinker."

"One does what one can," he said, bowing. "And you have to admit that I saved us a lot of time and effort."

I shrugged. "One would expect nothing less from a wizard."

We agreed to meet at the Matterhorn restaurant at a quarter to

eight and parted company when we reached Cameron's floor. The
cat went with him and I continued up to the next floor, wondering
if I'd have to spend the night in a hobbit-sized bed.

I was relieved to discover that my room had human-sized furniture
as well as a jacuzzi. The latter was useful in dispelling the scent of
dead trout, and a power nap ensured that I wouldn't doze off in the
midst of what might be a vitally important conversation. Though
the nap restored my energy, I elected to postpone calling Bill and
speaking with Aunt Dimity until after dinner, when I hoped to have
something substantive to tell them.

"If Bree is living with the Vclesuonnos," I said to Reginald, "you
and I will be heading home tomorrow."

As I left the room, I caught an inexplicable glint of disappointment in Reginald's black button eyes. My pink bunny, it seemed,
was in no hurry to return to the cottage. If I'd been perfectly hon-
est, I would have admitted that I wasn't, either. New Zealand, despite its manifold terrors, was beginning to grow on me.

The Matterhorn restaurant was spacious and full of character. Massive wood beams spanned the high, pine-clad ceiling, and rows
of tall windows reflected the soft light shed by the wrought-iron
chandeliers and wall sconces. The bar was inset with framed pieces
of marquetry depicting local scenes, and the lounge area was furnished with clusters of oversized leather armchairs and couches.
A log fire burned in the cylindrical brick-and-iron fireplace that
anchored the heart of the room.

I welcomed the fire's warmth. New Zealand's weather had

changed yet again and a cold fog had descended with nightfall. Although the restaurant was perfectly snug, the mere sight of chill mist clinging to the tall windows made me wish I'd worn my cashmere turtleneck instead of my silk blouse.

Cameron was waiting for me, slouched comfortably in an armchair near the fireplace with a glass of white wine in his hand. When he offered to order a drink for me, I declined. I wanted to be clearheaded when we spoke with Angelo.

"No stargazing tonight," I said, sinking into the armchair opposite his. "I seem doomed never to see the Southern Cross."

"I'll make sure you see it before you leave," Cameron promised. "We're bound to have at least one clear night." He lowered his voice and continued, "I've asked the maître d' to introduce us to the Velesuonnos. If all goes well, I'll invite them to dine with us."

I leaned back in my chair and studied him in silence.

"Why are you doing all of this?" I asked finally. "You don't know Ruth and Louise Pym, and you don't know me, yet you've gone to an insane amount of trouble to help us out. And don't tell me it's because you made a promise to an old school friend because I won't believe you. You've gone way beyond the call of *that* particular duty. So what's going on, Cameron? Is my husband blackmailing you? Do you owe him vast sums of money? Or are you just . . . incurably kindhearted?"

Cameron threw back his head and laughed. "To answer your last three questions: No, no, and certainly not."

"Since you haven't answered my first question, I'll ask it again," I said. "Why are you doing all of this?"

"I told you when we first met that I wished you could see more of my country," he replied. "Our merry chase has allowed me to show you a fair bit of it."

"Not good enough," I said flatly. "Try again."

"I'm having a wonderful time with you," he offered.

"Save the sweet talk for Teresa," I scolded. "Try again."

"Well . . ." He lowered his gray eyes to examine his fingernails. "I suppose it could have something to do with the day your husband saved my life."

My mouth fell open, but before I could do more than blink, a booming voice rang through the quiet restaurant.

"A fellow American? *Of course* she can join us for dinner! Lead us to her!"

The Velesuonnos had arrived.

Twelve

ngelo and Renee Velesuonno were originally from Yonkers, New York. They'd emigrated to New Zealand after falling in love with the country during a honeymoon tour of Australasia. They spent the winter months in Ohakune, where Angelo sold the best damned Buffalo chicken wings in the South Pacific while Renee worked as an oncology nurse at a hospital in nearby Waiouru. During the summer, they took time off to explore their adopted homeland.

It was a lot to learn within the first five minutes of meeting someone, but Angelo had retained a native New Yorker's habit of talking at the speed of light as well as his New York accent.

The Velesuonnos appeared to be in their early thirties. Renee was a full-figured woman whose wavy brown hair fell to her shoulders. She had hazel eyes, a fair complexion, and an acerbic wit that surfaced in a counterpoint commentary that accompanied her husband's tour-de-force introduction. She'd wisely donned a warm beige sweater and black trousers before venturing forth into the damp night.

Angelo wore a striped button-down shirt and white chinos. He had a small paunch—the result, I suspected, of a fondness for Buffalo chicken wings—and he'd shaved his black hair close to his scalp. His brown eyes were as appealing as a basset hound's and he was possibly the most hospitable man I'd ever met. As we took our seats at a table that had been hastily reset for four, he assured me that he and Renee *loved* meeting fellow Yanks, then waved off the menus and ordered dinner for all of us.

"Trust me, the duck is to die for," he told me, "and the venison is out of this world," he said to Cameron. "And don't even think about picking up the tab," he added firmly. "Dinner's on me. Where you from, Lori?"

"I was born and raised in Chicago," I said.

"I'm a Kiwi," Cameron put in. "Should I sit somewhere else?"

"A comedian," said Renee, rolling her eyes. "Just what I need, a Kiwi comic." She pointed a finger at Cameron. "Stay where you are, Mr. Funny."

"Yes, ma'am," he said.

"And don't *ma'am* me," she said, wagging a finger at him. "When I'm ninety you can *ma'am* me, but until then, I'm Renee."

"Yes, Renee," Cameron said meekly.

The wine arrived and Angelo launched into a panegyric about New Zealand sauvignon blanc that seemed to me to be entirely justified. I limited myself to a small sip, however. The night was young and I didn't want to lose focus. Something told me that it would take a fair amount of mental agility to get a word in edgewise with our genial host.

"What brings you to Ohakune?" Angelo asked, after Cameron and I had sampled the wine. "Hiking? Canoeing? Jet-boating? Spring skiing? Bird-watching?"

"None of the above," I replied. "We came here to find a young woman named Bree Pym."

"You hear that, Renee?" Angelo exclaimed. "How's that for a coincidence? The kid shows up on our doorstep after all this time and now Lori's asking about her." He leaned toward me. "How do you know her, Lori?"

"Her great-grandaunts are close friends of mine," I said. "They live in England and they've asked me to get in touch with Bree for them."

"Renee and I have known Bree since she was ten years old," he said.

"We spent six months in Takapuna," said Renee, "while Angelo set up his business—"

"Got a chain of cafés," Angelo interrupted. "They're eating my wings in Paihia, Auckland, Wellington, Nelson, Queenstown, *and* Dunedin. Can't get enough of them. Renee and me, we're making out like bandits."

"Angelo is the wing king," said Renee, bestowing a tolerant smile on her husband.

"If you have cafés all over New Zealand," I said, "why did you choose to live here? Didn't you realize how close you'd be to Mount Ruapehu?"

"Ohakune's a *great* place to live," said Angelo, slapping the table. "Not too big, not too small, and lots to do. And I'm telling you, Lori, we feel safer living next door to a volcano than we did walking down the street back home. There are too many angry people in the States and way too many guns."

"It's not a good combination," said Renee. "I should know. I'm a nurse."

"Here they use guns to kill possums and deer and wild pigs—not each other," Angelo went on. "And let me tell you, possums are a real problem in this country—they demolish native trees—so don't go feeling sorry for them."

Cameron made a gallant attempt to get the conversation back on track. "So you spent six months in Takapuna . . ."

"Rented a nice little beach house," said Angelo, without missing a beat, "right around the corner from the Pyms. Used to run into Bree all the time on her way home from school. Nice kid—good manners and sharp as a tack. We kept in touch with her for a while after we moved to Ohakune."

"What's all this about 'we'?" Renee demanded. "*I* was the one who kept in touch with her."

"And *I* kept in touch with her through *you*," her husband retorted. He turned back to me. "Her grandma died about a year after we left—God rest her soul—and we stopped hearing from Bree after that. You know how it is. Kids are so busy these days."

"Since when is a person too busy to send e-mail?" Renee grumbled. "It takes two seconds."

Angelo ignored her and continued talking to me. "You cannot imagine how shocked I was when Bree walked into the café, Lori. I'm telling you, I was *floored*."

Renee snorted derisively. "You didn't even know who she was until she told you."

"True," Angelo admitted. "Bree's not a little girl anymore, and when we lived in Takapuna, she didn't have short hair."

My eyebrows shot up. "Bree cut her hair?"

"It looks like she sawed through it with a butter knife," Renee informed me. "If she had it done at a salon, she could sue for damages."

"That's the style," Angelo objected. "It's cool."

"If looking like an escaped lunatic is cool, then her new hairstyle is cool," Renee conceded.

"Enough about her hair already," said Angelo, giving his wife an exasperated glare. "A girl like that, she could shave her head and she'd still be a knockout."

"Bree's a pretty girl," agreed Renee.

"She was looking for work," Angelo continued, "so we fixed her up with a job cleaning rooms at The Hobbit."

"The Hobbit?" I said.

"The Hobbit Motor Lodge," Renee clarified. "It's up the road. You passed it on your way to the Powderhorn."

"And let me point out that The Hobbit's been around for a long time," said Angelo. "The original owner was a Tolkien fan way before they started making these movies."

"A lot of us were," I said. I hesitated briefly, then asked, "Why didn't you give Bree a job at your café?"

"I had a full crew," Angelo replied. "Besides, the season was winding down. Renee and I were getting ready to close up shop here and head for our condo in Wellington."

"We like the theater," said Renee. "And the restaurants."

"And the museums and the night life," Angelo added.

"It makes a change from Ohakune," Renee concluded.

Two waitresses arrived with our dinners, sending Angelo into a spirited digression concerning the freshness of the locally grown produce and the rich flavors of the hormone-free meat.

"No hormones, no antibiotics, no factory farms," he said. "They don't mess with Mother Nature in New Zealand." He slapped the table again. "In this country, food tastes the way it's *supposed* to taste."

He waited until Cameron and I had tried each other's dishes and given them rave reviews—which was easy to do, because both the duck and the venison were sensational—before he returned to the topic of Bree.

"We let her use our guest room while she was here," he said. "To tell you the truth, we were a little concerned about her. She seemed kind of . . . moody." He paused to savor a forkful of caramelized leeks before going on. "When we asked how things were going in Takapuna, she didn't have much to say. Never talked about her grandpa or school or anything. She used to be as perky as a fantail, but now?" He shook his head. "Do you know what's up with her, Lori?"

"A lot," I said. "More than any eighteen-year-old should have to handle on her own. First of all, her grandfather died six weeks ago. . . ."

Angelo's expressive brown eyes became somber as I told him and Renee everything Cameron and I had learned about Bree's splintered family. When I finished, Renee folded her arms, tossed her head, and let out an explosive sigh.

"I *knew* it," she said. "I *knew* there was trouble at home. The minute I saw her hair, I knew there was trouble at home. Didn't I tell you there was trouble at home, Angelo?"

"You did," Angelo acknowledged. "Poor kid. Sounds like her dad was a real piece of work. He wasn't in the picture when we knew her. Just her grandma and grandpa."

"And she still doesn't know her dad's dead?" Renee inquired.

"Not unless she's gone back to Takapuna," I replied.

"She told Renee she'd *never* go back to Takapuna," Angelo informed me.

"Which is another reason I knew there was trouble at home," said Renee.

"She stayed with us for ten days," Angelo continued, "then she quit her job and took off for Wellington. That was about . . . what?" He glanced at his wife for confirmation. "Three weeks ago?"

"More like a month," Renee corrected him.

"She left with two Finnish girls she met at The Hobbit," said Angelo.

"Kitta and Kati," said Renee. "Ringers."

"Lord of the Rings fans," I said knowledgeably.

"Fanatics," Renee corrected me. "Do you know what they call Mount

Ngauruhoe? *Mount Doom*. And Ruapehu, according to them, is *Mordor*. I ask you. . . ." She clucked her tongue and peered heavenward.

"Kitta and Kati are hardcore Ringers," Angelo agreed. "The only reason they came to New Zealand was to visit movie locations. To tell you the truth, it's not a bad idea. The crazy director is using the whole country as a soundstage—North Island and South Island both. He's filming in all sorts of back-of-beyond places you'd never see on a normal tour."

"Kitta and Kati have seen more of New Zealand than we have," Renee added.

Angelo nodded. "When they were done climbing around on Ruapehu—"

"Mordor," Renee interjected, rolling her eyes.

"—they headed for the film studios down in Wellington," Angelo went on, "and Bree tagged along with them. We gave her a few bucks and told her to have a good time. It beats scrubbing toilets, and if you don't have fun when you're young—"

"—you'll have fun later on and your husband won't like it," said Renee.

I groaned. "We'll never be able to find Bree in Wellington. It's a big city, isn't it?"

"It's the capital city," said Angelo. "But New York it isn't. And we can tell you exactly where the girls are staying because we gave them the keys to our place."

I blinked at him, nonplussed. "You gave three teenaged girls the keys to your condo?"

"Kitta and Kati aren't teenagers," said Renee. "If you ask me, they're a little long in the tooth to be chasing elves, but"—she shrugged—"to each her own."

"They're nice women," Angelo declared. "Sure, they're a little whacky when it comes to Tolkien, but they've got their feet on the ground. We wouldn't have encouraged Bree to go with them if we thought they were bad news."

"We rent out the condo in the winter," said Renee, "but our tenants left early, so we figured, why not let the girls use it? It's better to have someone there than to leave the place empty."

"And it beats sleeping on a park bench," Angelo put in.

"Have you been in touch with Bree since she left?" I asked.

Angelo shook his head. "You know how it is. When a girl's having fun, she doesn't stop to think that people might want to hear from her."

"Have you tried calling her?" I asked.

"Can't," said Renee. "We don't have phone service at the condo."

"Renee and I use cell phones," said Angelo. "You'd think Bree would have one, wouldn't you? Most kids walk around with cell phones glued to their ears these days, but not Bree."

"She probably can't afford one," I said. "Her father liked to gamble."

"A real piece of work," said Angelo, pursing his lips in disgust. "Bree deserves better than that."

"Her great-grandaunts are two of the finest people you could ever hope to meet," I assured him. "I think it would give Bree a boost to know that a pair of little old ladies in England care very much about her."

"It couldn't hurt," said Angelo. "So you're going to Wellington?"

"No other choice," I replied. "I just hope she's still using your condo."

Renee pulled a pen and a pad of paper out of her purse. "I'll give you the address and our phone numbers. Call us when you get there, will you?"

"Of course," I said.

"If we'd known Bree was in trouble," Angelo said soberly, "we would have done more for her. But you know how it is. If a kid doesn't want you to know something, you're not going to know it." He waved the waitress over, ordered English toffee pudding with custard for all of us, and sat back as she began clearing the table. "So, where have you two been so far?"

The Velesuonnos regaled us with travel stories until eleven o'clock, when I could no longer keep my eyelids from drooping. We thanked them for a splendid dinner, walked them to the chateau's main entrance, and waved good-bye as they disappeared into the fog.

"What's a fantail?" I asked Cameron as we strolled across the lobby.

"A chatty little bird," he replied. "If you ever hike through a New Zealand forest, chances are a fantail will accompany you. They flit around like fairies, eating the bugs stirred up by hiking boots. Very personable. Very cute."

"Sounds like it," I said, and as we waited for the elevator, I found myself wishing that we could stay in Ohakune long enough to explore the forest cloaking Mount Ruapehu's lower slopes. It would be worth the risk, I thought, to have a chatty little bird flit around me like a fairy while we hiked.

"Bree's hair worries me," said Cameron.

"Me, too," I said, coming out of my reverie. "If you ask me, she chopped it off because she doesn't want to look like her mother."

"If so, she's rejecting her mother by disfiguring herself," he said. "It's a self-destructive act. Do you remember what Alison said to us at the Copthorne?"

"Alison, the waitress?" I asked after a moment's thought.

Cameron nodded. "She said, 'Someone needs to find that girl

before she does something stupid.' I thought she was being melo-dramatic, but after hearing about Bree's hair, I'm not so sure. She's cut her hair. What if she cuts herself next?"

We stood aside as an elderly couple tottered slowly out of the elevator. As we stepped aboard, the hotel cat appeared out of no-where, darted into the elevator with us, and proceeded to polish Cameron's shoes with her head. I wondered fleetingly if the cat's name was Teresa.

"Bree must have a lot of anger bottled up inside her," Cameron said. "If you ask me, she's a ticking time bomb. We have to find her before she explodes."

"Wellington tomorrow," I said. "It's the best lead we've had yet."

"Can you be ready to leave by nine?" he asked.

I nodded. I would have preferred to stay in bed until noon the next day, but I told myself that I could catch up on sleep as soon as we'd caught up with Bree.

Cameron and the cat left the elevator when we reached his floor, but as the door began to slide shut, I stuck my hand out to stop it and hopped into the hallway after them.

"Wait a minute," I said in an urgent whisper. "How did my hus-band save your life?"

"Ask him," Cameron replied. He smiled enigmatically, leaned past me to push the call button, and strode down the dim, plaid-carpeted corridor, with the cat padding faithfully at his heels.

"You bet I will," I murmured, gazing at their retreating backs.

"And *Bill* told me to ask *Cameron*," I grumbled.

An hour had passed since Cameron and I had gone our separate ways. I'd spoken with Bill after returning to my room, then changed into my nightgown and climbed into bed with the blue journal. Although I was more tired than I'd ever been in my life, sheer frustration was keeping me awake. I tossed my head scornfully as Aunt Dimity's handwriting scrolled across the page.

Men aren't like women, Lori. They tend to be reticent about personal experiences, especially if the experience in question involves an element of heroism.

"Are you trying to tell me that men don't brag?" I demanded.

Adolescents brag, Lori. Mature men don't feel the need to advertise their good deeds. I'm happy to say that you are married to a very mature man.

"Mature? Ha!" I snarled. "Bill isn't being mature, Dimity. He's having a little fun at my expense. He *knows* how much I hate puzzles. He and Camo are behaving like a pair of schoolboys, keeping secrets and giggling behind my back."

Bill and Cameron were schoolboys together. I suppose they could be regressing.

"It's like having an itch I can't scratch," I seethed.

I'm certain that they'll tell you the whole story eventually. In the meantime, try to focus on Bree's problems, which are far more serious than your own. I must say that I agree with Cameron's assessment of the situation. The child seems to be in a very fragile state.

"If the child would sit still for two minutes, I might be able to help her," I said. "But until she stays put long enough for Cameron and me to pin her down, there's not a darned thing I can do about her fragile state."

Concentrate, then, on Bill's splendid news. Dr. Finisterre has taken Ruth and Louise off oxygen. Nell's nursing and their fascination with your journey have given them a new lease on life. You've made a significant con-

tribution to their unanticipated progress, Lori. It must warm your heart to know that they've regained some of their strength.

"It's the best news I've heard since they fell ill," I acknowledged.

And think of how much you've learned about the New Zealand branch of the Pym family.

"Hold on a minute," I said. I looked up from the journal and peered intently into the middle distance. Aunt Dimity's words had triggered a memory, but I needed a moment to capture it. "Amanda said something strange this morning, Dimity. I'd forgotten about it until now, when you mentioned the New Zealand branch of the Pym family."

What did Amanda say?

I glanced down at the journal, then looked away again, frowning in concentration. "She said that, when Ed Pym was drunk, he'd talk about 'the English aunts.' He 'cursed them'—those were her words," I went on, nodding. "Amanda thought he was delusional."

A reasonable assumption, given his inebriated state.

"He wasn't delusional, though, was he?" I said. "He must have been referring to Ruth and Louise."

He may have heard his father speak of them.

"Okay," I said slowly. "So Aubrey Pym, Senior, tells his son A. J. about the twin sisters he left behind in England. And A. J. passes the story along to *his* son, Ed. And Ed ends up cursing the English aunts. What story did Ed hear, Dimity? What made him think that Ruth and Louise were the bad guys?"

As I've indicated before, family feuds can span many generations.

"Yes," I said, "but Aubrey's dispute was with his father, not with his sisters. Ruth and Louise didn't kick him out of the house. His father did. I could understand it if he told nasty stories about his dear old dad, but why would he paint his sisters as villains? They'd done nothing to harm him. They were innocent bystanders in the whole affair."

Perhaps the story became garbled as it was passed down from father to son.

"Or from father to daughter," I said. "I wonder what Bree knows, or *thinks* she knows, about her great-grandaunts?"

I expect you'll find out when you and Cameron reach Wellington.

"I expect so," I said, "unless Bree has taken off for Rio or Nairobi or Minneapolis. . . ."

I sincerely doubt that Bree can afford to go to any of those places. Have faith, Lori. You will find her. Good night, my dear.

"Good night."

I watched Aunt Dimity's handwriting fade from the page, placed the journal on the bedside table, twiddled Reginald's ears, and turned out the light. As I snuggled my head into the pillows, however, a small part of my brain was still chattering away like a fantail.

How would Bree react to the Pym sisters' letter? I asked myself. Would she rip it to shreds, or weep tears of joy over it?

And how, I wondered, had my husband saved Cameron's life?

Thirteen

The fog had lifted by the time I met Cameron for breakfast in the Matterhorn the following morning. When we checked out of the hotel, Teresa urged us to return soon and to stay longer. I responded with a courteous nod, even though I was dead certain that she wasn't talking to me.

I was faintly shocked when the hotel cat failed to follow us to the jeep. Eau de Cameron combined with the fragrance of dead trout should have been irresistible to her, but she stayed in her grotto, intent, no doubt, on seducing the next good-looking stranger who walked into the chateau.

It took us a little over an hour to drive back to the Taupo airport, where Aidan Dun was waiting for us, clad in brown corduroy trousers, a green oiled-cotton jacket, and a beat-up straw cowboy hat decorated with fishing lures. I shared the last of the Anzac biscuits with him—they didn't seem to get stale—and we shot the breeze while Cameron refueled the plane.

"Has Cameron ever told you a story about someone saving his life?" I asked.

"Sure," said Aidan. "He claims that Donna saved his life when she married him."

My spirits, which had risen briefly, settled back into their original, frustrated position.

"Just his wife?" I pressed. "No one else?"

Aidan tilted his cowboy hat back and rubbed his jaw thoughtfully as he mulled over the question.

"I hauled him away from a bar fight once," he said finally. "If Donna ever found out that he'd been stupid enough to get himself into a bar fight, she'd kill him, so I guess you could say *I* saved his life."

I forced a smile, bit into my cookie, and chewed. It was healthier than grinding my teeth.

My prickly mood vanished as soon as Cameron and I were airborne. It was impossible to remain irritable while gazing down on the sparkling waters of Lake Taupo and the strange, crinkled landscape of Tongariro National Park. As we flew farther south, Cameron pointed out the green spines of the Ruahine and the Tararua ranges to the east and the telltale cone shape of Mount Taranaki to the west. He also drew my attention to a variegated patch of green in the Tasman Sea.

"Kapiti Island," he informed me. "It's a nature reserve. More of an ark, really. It's the last best hope on earth for some of our most endangered species."

I enjoyed the flight so thoroughly that I felt a jab of disappointment when he informed me that we were about to land. I was also confused. Although Angelo had described Wellington as a small city, I was certain that it had to be bigger than the farmstead Cameron was circling.

"Where's Wellington?" I asked.

"About fifty kilometers farther south," he said. "We'll leave the plane here and drive into town."

"I get it," I said, as understanding dawned. "Whose car are we borrowing this time?"

"Mine," said Cameron. "Hold on tight, Lori. You're about to experience your first paddock landing."

I had no time to panic or to plead with him to find a paved runway. One minute we were in the air and the next we were bouncing along the grass in the center of a fenced field. The bounces were surprisingly gentle and we seemed to have plenty of room, so on the whole I preferred the paddock landing to the one we'd made on the shores of Lake Taupo.

"Well done," I said, when the plane came to a halt.

"Thanks," he said. "I've had a fair amount of practice landing in this particular paddock because I live here. Well, actually . . ." He pointed to a large and handsome one-story brick house a few hundred yards away from us. "I live *there*."

I unbuckled my seat belt in record time, lowered myself onto the grass without Cameron's assistance, and took a good look at my surroundings. Although I was anxious to get to Wellington, I wasn't about to waste a golden opportunity to see the place my native guide called home.

Cameron's house stood on a rise with its back to a range of rolling green hills, facing acres of tree-fringed fields that sloped gradually down to the sea. Dozens of exquisite horses grazed or galloped in the verdant pastures adjacent to the one in which we'd landed. The pastureland was dotted with tiny yellow flowers, and Kapiti Island floated offshore, swathed in a faint haze that made it appear dramatically remote and mysterious.

Cameron hopped out of the plane, retrieved our bags, and came to stand beside me.

"Will and Rob would go googly over this place," I said. "A horse-filled pasture is their idea of paradise."

"You'll have to bring them with you next time." He pointed to a dense avenue of trees to our right. "The stables and the training facilities are behind the shelterbelt."

"What's a shelterbelt?" I asked.

"A really big hedgerow," he answered, grinning. "The trees protect my outbuildings from the gales that blow in off the Tassie." He swept an arm through the air to indicate pretty much every square inch of land in sight. "My property runs from the hills down to the sea. Nice view, eh?"

"*Nice?*" I cried. "Cameron, the view is *astounding*."

"It's all right," he said with a diffident shrug. "Come on. Donna's waiting for us."

I followed him through a gate in the two-bar wooden fence surrounding the field and up a dirt driveway to his house. We'd scarcely set foot on the verandah when the front door opened and a frisky black-and-white Jack Russell terrier scampered outside to greet us.

Close on the terrier's heels came a diminutive, dark-haired woman who appeared to be in her early thirties. She was dressed in jeans, a navy blue track jacket, and white sweat socks, and she carried a duffel bag similar to Cameron's. While the dog sniffed his master's cat-scented shoes, the woman stood on tiptoe to give Cameron a peck on the cheek, then nodded to me.

"Donna Mackenzie," she said.

"Lori Shepherd," I responded. "Thank you so much for the Anzac biscuits. I hope you won't mind if I pester you for the recipe. My sons will gobble them up."

"I'll e-mail it to Bill," she said, smiling. "As a matter of fact, he sent an e-mail to me this morning, to give to you." She handed me a white business envelope addressed to Aubrey Aroha Pym. "It's a letter," she explained, "from the Pym sisters to their great-grandniece."

"They must be feeling better, if they're dictating letters," I marveled, slipping the envelope into my day pack. "Thanks a lot, Donna."

"No worries," she said. "Cam's told me what you're doing and I think it's fantastic."

"I'm sorry it's taking so long," I said.

"Take as long as you like," she said, waving aside my apology. "It'd be a shame to come all this way for nothing. Besides, Cam needs a break. *Stay right where you are*," she growled at her husband, who'd been sidling furtively toward the door.

Though soft-spoken and small of stature, Donna had the command presence of a five-star general. Cameron froze as if he'd been zapped by a stun gun and peered timidly at his wife. The Velesuonnos, it seemed, weren't the only ones living near an active volcano.

"Donna," he began.

She overrode him. "If I let you into the house, you'll take one look at the week's schedule and go straight back to work. Do you want Lori to *walk* to Wellington?"

"No, but—"

"Do you want to break your promise to Bill?" she demanded.

"No, but—"

"Then *stay where you are*." Donna folded her arms and glared at her husband, then appealed to me. "Cam hasn't taken a day off since they started making those Lord of the Rings films. He's *earned* a holiday."

A devilish smile curved my lips as I glanced at Cameron, whose face had turned crimson.

"Your husband didn't tell me that he was involved in the films," I said.

"He's not," said Donna, "but every other professional horseman in New Zealand *is*. When they ran off with the circus, their regular clients came running to us. Cam's never been busier. He's training horses, instructing riders, flying all over the country to judge competitions. . . . He's working himself to death while his mates are prancing around in capes and wigs and armor and I-don't-know-what. If he doesn't slow down, he'll end up in hospital." She cast a fierce, protective glance at her husband. "Well, I won't have it. His crew can manage without him for a few days, whatever he may think. He *needs* a break."

"I understand," I said, and I truly did. Bill's work ethic was, alas, very similar to Cameron's.

"I've made reservations for you at the Copthorne on Oriental Parade," Donna said to her husband. "If you need the plane, Trevor can fly it down to you. I've packed enough clean clothes to last a week." She exchanged her duffel bag for Cameron's, then pointed imperiously to the attached garage. "Get in your car and go, Cam. I don't want to see you back here until you've done what you set out to do. Nice to meet you, Lori. Good luck finding Bree!"

She kissed her husband, scooped up the exuberant terrier, went back into the house, and slammed the door. A moment later, the garage door swung open. Cameron heaved a heavy sigh and trudged toward it. I took a last look at the misty outline of Kapiti Island and followed him.

Cameron's black Land Rover looked as though it had been driven through every mud puddle in New Zealand, its seats were liberally sprinkled with wisps of straw, and it exuded a bouquet of fragrances I normally associated with horses, but it didn't stink of fish. As an added attraction, a shiny, chintz-patterned biscuit tin sat on the dusty dashboard. A peek inside confirmed my suspicion that Donna had baked a fresh batch of cookies for us.

I clambered into the passenger seat and swapped the full tin for the empty one in my day pack while Cameron deposited our duffel bags in the back. When he slid into the driver's seat, I nudged him with my elbow.

"Are you okay?" I asked.

"Considering the fact that my wife has just given me a royal bollicking," he said, "I'm not doing too badly."

"It's none of my business," I said, "but she does seem to have your best interests at heart. She wants you to take a break because she loves you."

"I know." He rested his hands on the steering wheel and stared pensively through the windshield. "But there's no need for her to act as though I'm the only responsible horseman in New Zealand. Film work isn't as easy as Donna makes out, Lori. It's a demanding, difficult, and dangerous job. It takes expert riders to pull it off without injuring themselves or their horses. I have nothing but respect for the men and women who are working on the Ring trilogy. They're earning their pay."

"So are you," I said. "If everyone traded real life for the movies, who would teach the police commissioner's granddaughter how to ride?"

Cameron managed a weak smile.

"Listen," I said, pivoting to face him. "If you have more important things to do—"

"Forget it," he interrupted. "If I go back to work right now, Donna will chop me into little pieces and feed me to the dog." He straightened his shoulders, lifted his chin, and turned the key in the ignition. "Next stop, *Wellington*."

Fourteen

Our next stop was, in fact, Paekakariki, a seaside village with a long, sandy beach, a multitude of art studios, and a café where we ate lunch before hitting the road again. We reached New Zealand's capital at two o'clock.

After spending so much time in rural settings, it was a bit jarring to enter a distinctly urban environment, but Wellington, as Angelo had intimated, was not New York. Though its suburbs crept outward in a far-reaching sprawl, the city proper was amazingly compact, nestled snugly between steep, heavily forested hills and a massive bay known, appropriately, as Wellington Harbor.

There weren't many tall buildings, and even the tallest didn't come close to scraping the sky. Wellingtonians lived as well as worked in the center of town, where modern glass-and-steel office blocks rubbed shoulders with Victorian holdouts housing an eclectic collection of cafés, restaurants, bookstores, and funky boutiques. The sidewalks and bike paths were crowded with so many young people that we could have been driving through a college campus.

Cameron, who knew the city well, identified various places of interest along the way, the most striking of which was the Beehive, a bristling, dome-shaped edifice that housed New Zealand's parliament. I didn't care for the Beehive, but I was drawn to Te Papa, the Museum of New Zealand, which brightened the waterfront with its colors, its curves, and its angles. Te Papa, I thought, had been designed by someone who knew how to throw a good party.

"What does Te Papa mean?" I asked while we waited in front of the museum for a traffic light to change.

"It's short for Te Papa Tongarewa," Cameron replied. "It's a Maori phrase, of course, and an extremely literal translation would be . . ." He took a deep breath before reciting, " 'Our well-loved repository and showcase of treasured things and people that spring from Mother Earth here in New Zealand.' "

"Wow," I said, impressed. "I can see why they use the Maori phrase. They'd have a hard time cramming the English version onto a bumper sticker." The traffic light turned green and we pulled away from the museum. "I assume we're going straight to the condo."

"Faulty assumption," said Cameron. "We're not in Ohakune anymore, Lori. It makes more sense to leave the car at the hotel and walk than it does to waste time hunting for a parking space near the condo."

Approximately two seconds later, he handed his car keys to a valet while a bellman placed our bags on a luggage cart. We'd arrived at our second Copthorne Hotel.

The Wellington branch of the Copthorne chain occupied a prime chunk of waterfront real estate directly across the street from a marina and a stone's throw away from Te Papa. The ten-story building had clean, contemporary lines inside and out. My room had been decorated by a minimalist with a passion for soft lighting, silky textures, and practical details. Walking into it was like entering a well-designed cocoon, and its miniscule balcony afforded me fabulous views of the city as well as the bay.

Donna had evidently chosen the hotel for its strategic location as well as its amenities, because the address Renee had given us belonged to a nondescript, eight-story box of a building less than two blocks away from the Copthorne. I would have preferred living in one of the pastel-colored Victorian gems we passed on our way to the condo, but the lovingly restored little houses probably required more upkeep than part-time residents like the Velesuonnos were willing to give them.

We let ourselves into the nondescript box's lobby and Cameron pressed the buzzer labeled VELESUONNO. A moment later a voice crackled through the intercom. The voice belonged to a woman who spoke with an accent, but unfortunately, she sounded more like a Finn than a Kiwi.

"Who is it, please?" she asked.

"Lori Shepherd and Cameron Mackenzie," I replied, speaking slowly and distinctly. "Angelo and Renee sent us."

"Oh." A long pause ensued before the voice added hesitantly, "Come up. We're at the top floor."

The inner door clicked and we walked through another lobby to board an elevator, which took us to a small, windowless foyer on the eighth floor, where a woman stood, waiting for us.

She definitely wasn't Bree Pym. Bree was petite, but this woman was downright tiny. She was also a lot older than Bree—in her late thirties rather than her late teens. Her disheveled, pale blond hair framed a weather-beaten and deeply tanned face, and she was dressed like a latter-day hippie, in embroidered jeans, an embroidered denim waistcoat, and a frilly white cotton blouse that fell almost to her knees. A tiny book bound in red paper hung from a gold cord around her neck.

"Kati Malinen," she said, shaking our hands.

Though Kati smiled enchantingly as Cameron and I introduced ourselves, I detected a hint of nervousness in her blue eyes.

"We're not kicking you out of the condo," I assured her.

"And we're not here to inspect it," Cameron hastened to add.

Kati's nervousness gave way to polite perplexity. "Why are you here, then?"

"We need to speak with Bree Pym," I said.

"Oh." Kati's broad smile wavered. "Are you the police?"

"The police?" I said, my heart plummeting. "Why would the police want to speak with Bree?"

"Well," she said, "Roger said he would not press charges, but he could have changed his mind."

"Who is Roger?" I asked.

"Roger is a very great tattoo artist," Kati informed me earnestly.

"What?" I said, utterly at sea.

"Perhaps we should sit down," Cameron suggested.

"Yes, of course," said Kati, nodding. "Please, come inside."

We followed her into a stylishly appointed open-plan penthouse with views of the bay and the city that rivaled those I'd observed from my balcony at the Copthorne. The walls were white, the carpeting was sand-colored, and the furnishings were made principally of teak, leather, and chrome.

The condo's most arresting feature was the woman who stood in the middle of the living room area, clutching an overflowing laundry basket to her chest. To judge by her guilty expression, the faint sheen of perspiration on her forehead, and the odd assortment of items in her basket—socks, bras, dishes, books, sneakers—she'd spent the past few minutes making a heroic attempt to tidy the place before Cameron and I walked into it.

Kati gestured toward the woman.

"My friend, Kitta Lehtonen," she said to us. She added something in Finnish, whereupon Kitta grunted, dropped the laundry basket, and collapsed into a teak-and-leather chair, fanning herself.

Kitta was taller and lankier than Kati, and less inclined to smile, but she, too, looked as though she might be in her late thirties. Her face was round, her complexion pale, and she wore her brown hair in two shiny braids that fell past her waist. She was dressed more prosaically than Kati, in a bright blue scoop-necked top and unadorned jeans. The dark green pendant resting between her collar bones was similar to those worn by Toko Baker and Amanda Rivers, a flat disk with a graceful scroll carved at its center, like a breaking wave.

"Jade?" I asked, pointing to the pendant.

"Pounamu," she replied. "Also called greenstone. Greenstone is a jade found only in New Zealand. It is carved into a koru," she added, touching a fingertip to the pendant.

"A koru is an opening fern frond," Cameron interjected. "It's a symbol of new life and new beginnings."

"And a newly cleaned flat," said Kati, laughing. "Please, sit. Would you like something to drink? We have juice, bottled water, wine, beer . . ."

"Nothing for me, thank you," Cameron and I chorused.

Kati motioned for us to be seated on the leather couch, whisked the laundry basket into another room, and curled up in a chair opposite Kitta's.

"We were afraid you would report our bad housekeeping to Angelo and Renee," she said, her eyes dancing.

"We're not spies," I told her. "We're just trying to find Bree."

"Bree?" said Kitta, sitting upright. "You know Bree?"

"Sort of," I said. "I'm a family friend."

"You will report her to her family?" Kitta asked, her eyes narrowing suspiciously.

"I won't report Bree to *anyone*," I said, exasperated. "I have a message to deliver to her, that's all. Can you tell me where she is?"

"She left Wellington ten days ago," said Kati, "after the trouble with Roger."

"What kind of trouble?" Cameron asked.

Kati and Kitta exchanged uncomfortable looks.

"It started well," Kitta stated, as though she felt the need to justify herself. "For two weeks, Bree had fun."

"Right away she gets a job at the Chocolate Fish," said Kati.

Cameron noticed my puzzled expression and explained, "The Chocolate Fish is a café frequented by the younger actors in the Lord of the Rings movies."

"On her days off she comes with us to the hills above the film studios," said Kati. "It is exciting to look down on the sets and the actors."

"Exciting, but not allowed," said Kitta. "Security chased us away."

"But we go back," said Kati, grinning mischievously. "We hide behind trees and look through bushes. Bree likes this very much. She had fun."

"What happened?" I asked. "How did Bree go from having fun to being in trouble?"

Kati gave Kitta a sidelong glance, then said, "Bree came with us when we get our tattoos."

She pulled up her pant leg to reveal a circle of unfamiliar but elegant script tattooed in black ink just above her left ankle. Simultaneously, Kitta held up her arm to display a "bracelet" of the same script inked around her wrist.

"Finnish?" I inquired.

"Elvish," Kitta replied. "The words are private. Please do not ask me to translate."

"Wouldn't dream of it," Cameron murmured.

"We want a special thing to remind us of our time here in Middle Earth," said Kati, referring to the imaginary world in which Tolkien's tales were set.

"Also to remind us of the Maori," Kitta added.

"Tattoos play an important role in Maori culture," Cameron said to me. "Remember Toko?"

I nodded as I recalled Toko Baker's legs, covered from ankle to thigh with an intricate pattern of tattoos.

"I think I understand," I said, looking from Kitta to Kati. "Middle Earth and New Zealand come together in your elvish tattoos."

"Exactly right," said Kati, beaming at me.

"Bree also wants a tattoo, but not elvish," said Kitta. "She gets an owl on her shoulder. She says it is her Ruru."

"Ruru is the Maori name for the morepork owl," Cameron elucidated. "It's one of the few native species that isn't endangered."

"It is the name also for her little friend," Kitta said. "Her—" She broke off and looked to Kati for guidance. "How do you call it?"

"Her soft toy," Kati put in.

I had a sudden vision of the stuffed animals in Bree's bedroom and the indentation I'd noticed on her pillow. Had the dent marked the spot where Ruru had lain before she'd tucked him into her backpack and set out on her seemingly endless journey?

"She first gets the owl tattoo," Kati continued. "Then she gets a flower."

"Then more flowers." Kitta tapped two fingers along her arm, from her wrist to her shoulder. "Flowers, all up her arms."

"One day Roger tells her she must stop because it is too much, too fast," said Kati.

"It is not good to go so fast with tattoos," said Kitta severely.

"Roger tells her, slow down," said Kati, "and Bree . . ." She lowered her eyes and shook her head sadly.

"Bree goes crazy," Kitta declared, pursing her lips. "She shouts at Roger. She breaks his lamp." She pointed to her eyes. "She *breaks his glasses.*"

"How can Roger work without his glasses?" Kati asked with a helpless shrug. "But Roger is a good man—as wise as a wizard and as noble as an elf-lord. He does not call the police."

"We bring Bree home," said Kitta. "She cries and cries."

"And next morning," said Kati, "she is gone."

The two friends fell silent. I leaned my forehead on my hands, feeling heartsick. It sounded as though Cameron's prediction had come true: The ticking time bomb had finally exploded. I was certain that, had it not been for Roger's extraordinary forbearance, Bree's actions would have landed her in jail.

"Do you know where she went?" Cameron asked.

"No," said Kati. "She goes before we are awake and she does not leave a note."

"Does she still have her car?" he asked.

"Yes, of course," said Kitta. "The Chocolate Fish is in Scorching Bay. She needs her car to work there."

Cameron glanced speculatively toward the kitchen. "Was Bree drunk when she had her row with Roger?"

I raised my head, half afraid to hear the answer.

"Oh, no," Kati said earnestly. "Bree does not drink."

"Not even wine," Kitta added.

I breathed a sigh of relief. The years Bree had spent with her father had, it seemed, taught her the folly of seeking solace in a bottle.

"We'll pay for Roger's glasses and his lamp," said Cameron. He took his wallet from his pocket and passed a handful of bills to Kati. "Please tell him how grateful we are to him for his kindness to Bree."

"I will," said Kati.

A cell phone rang. I looked around expectantly until it dawned on me that the sound was coming from my day pack. A sense of foreboding crept over me as I fished the phone out of my pack. It could only be Bill, I thought, calling to tell me that Ruth and Louise were dead.

"Hello?" I said.

"Hey, Lori! How's it shakin'?"

Angelo Velesuonno's voice had never sounded so sweet. If he'd been within arm's reach, I would have kissed him.

"Angelo!" I exclaimed. "Guess what? Cameron and I are sitting in your condo right now, talking with Kati and Kitta. Unfortunately, Bree's not with us. She left the condo ten days ago."

"I know," he said. "I just got a call from one of my managers. He tells me that a girl filled out a job application last week, using my name as a reference. He wanted to know if I knew a Bree Pym. Can you believe it? I told him to chain her to the fryer, but he tells me that she hasn't been back since she filled out the application. He's seen her around town, though, so he thinks she got a job somewhere else."

"Which café are you talking about, Angelo?" I asked. "Where is it?"

"Queenstown," he said. "Renee and I have condo down there, too. We'd offer it to you, but we rented it out to a nice Australian family. If you run into the Robbins while you're there, tell 'em we said g'day!"

"Will do," I said. "Thanks for letting us know about Bree."

"No problem," he said. "Renee and I want what's best for her. Tell the Kiwi comic to keep the laughs coming. And stay in touch!"

"You bet I will." I rang off, dropped the phone into my pack, and announced to the room at large: "Bree is in Queenstown."

Cameron pulled out his cell phone and began punching keys.

"We'll need the plane," he said to me. "Queenstown is on the South Island. Bree probably took the ferry and drove the rest of the way, but you and I will fly."

Kati's face lit up. "You will find Bree?"

"Yes," Cameron replied determinedly. "We will find Bree."

"Fantastic," she said.

She hopped out of her chair again and left the living room. A moment later she returned, cradling a small and very bedraggled stuffed animal in her hands. The little owl had golden eyes, a honey-colored face, and mottled brown-and-gold markings all over his fluffy wings and body.

"Bree forgot Ruru," said Kati. "You can bring him to her. I think she needs him."

"I think so, too," I said, and while Cameron arranged for his airplane to be flown to Wellington the following morning, I opened my day pack and gently tucked Ruru in beside Reginald.

Fifteen

In keeping with the avian theme my trip had suddenly acquired, Cameron and I had dinner at The Green Parrot, a noisy, lively restaurant that was, he assured me, a Wellington institution. We sat beneath a huge mural depicting well-known customers and watched as passersby had their pictures taken beside the parrot-shaped, pink-and-green neon sign.

The food was excellent—I had the scallops, Cameron, the sirloin steak, and we shared a dozen oysters—but I was relieved when we finished the meal and returned to the hotel. I longed to speak to Bill, and I had an awful lot to discuss with Aunt Dimity.

"Bill?" I said as soon as I heard his voice. "Let's never become drunk, lazy, lying, gambling losers, okay?"

"Okay," he replied readily.

"And let's *never* get divorced," I went on.

"Sounds good to me," he said.

"And let's *always* treat Rob and Will like the little miracles they are," I continued fervently.

"Your little miracles drew dinosaurs on the kitchen wall last night," Bill said grimly, "with black shoe polish."

"We can paint over it," I said.

"Do you know how many coats of primer it takes to cover black shoe polish? *I* do." He grumbled indistinctly for a moment, then took a cleansing breath and asked calmly, "What's going on, Lori? Why are you so spooked?"

"It's Bree," I said. I told him about Bree's worrisome addiction to tattoos, her run-in with Roger, and her unannounced departure from Wellington. "She didn't stop to say good-bye to Kati and Kitta, and she really seemed to like them. I don't think she knows where she's going or what she's looking for, Bill. She's just . . . running."

"She's too young to know that you can't outrun your past," said Bill. "And her past is pretty messed up."

"That's my point," I said. "Let's give our children a past they won't *want* to outrun."

"If they use shoe polish on the walls again, I'll give them a past they'll never forget," Bill growled.

"How are Ruth and Louise?" I asked hastily, hoping to distract him from the shoe polish incident.

"They're not tap dancing yet, but they've penciled it into their schedules," he replied. "They're doing remarkably well, Lori. Dr. Finisterre is baffled but delighted, as are we all. Did Donna Mackenzie give you the letter I e-mailed for them?"

"It's in my day pack," I said. "I'll deliver it to Bree as soon as Cameron and I catch up with her."

"Aren't you going to quiz me about the letter?" Bill asked, sounding faintly disappointed.

"No," I replied. "It's a private matter between Bree and her great-grandaunts. I will, however, jump up and down on your head if you don't tell me how you saved Cameron's life."

"Since my head is here and your feet are there," said Bill, "I feel safe in saying, yet again, that it's Cameron's story to tell."

I wheedled, scolded, and coaxed, but he steadfastly refused to discuss the matter, so I let it go. After sending kisses to the boys and love to Willis, Sr., I said good night to my no-good rat of a husband, plugged the cell phone into the charger, and climbed into bed with the blue journal.

I allowed myself a sixty-second rant about Bill's juvenile sense of humor, then settled down to tell Aunt Dimity about Bree's ill-fated stay in Wellington.

"First she cuts her hair," I said, echoing words Cameron had spoken the previous evening, "then she cuts herself or allows Roger-the-very-great-tattoo-artist to cut her. Heaven knows what she's done to herself by now."

She may not have done anything, Lori. She released a flood of pent-up anger at the tattoo parlor and she cried herself to sleep afterward. Catharsis is good for the soul, my dear. I wish most sincerely that Bree's catharsis hadn't come at the expense of poor Roger's glasses, but it may have been just what she needed to steady herself. She may be all right for a while.

"If Bree felt better after her meltdown, why didn't she say goodbye to Kati and Kitta?" I asked. "Why did she just duck out on them? She didn't even leave them a note."

I suspect that Bree was too ashamed of herself to face her friends, even in writing, which indicates to me that her conscience is still functioning. Furthermore, her refusal to sedate herself with alcohol argues for a strong sense of self-preservation. A girl her age and in her situation might be sorely tempted to drown her sorrows at the nearest pub, but Bree has so far displayed no inclination to test her mettle against the brutal disease that killed her father. Surely these are hopeful signs.

"Don't the tattoos bother you?" I asked.

Not in the least. Bree was born and raised in New Zealand, where tattoos are as common as sheep. I might have been alarmed if she'd decided to decorate her body with skulls or satanic symbols, but she chose flowers. As rebellious acts go, having oneself tattooed with flowers is fairly harmless.

"What about leaving Ruru behind?" I looked at Reginald, who sat on the bedside table, gazing amiably at his new acquaintance. "I'd have to be in a terrible state to forget Reg."

Bree IS in a terrible state. Catharsis may be good for the soul, but it isn't a cure-all, Lori. Bree's troubles are far from over, but I do not believe that she is in imminent danger of harming herself irretrievably. Her mind must have been in a whirl when she fled the condo. I'm certain that she suffered pangs of remorse when she discovered Ruru's absence. Fortunately, she has a ruru tattooed on her shoulder.

"A tattoo is no substitute for a soft, fluffy owl," I said.

Perhaps not, but I learned from one of my Kiwi soldiers that the Maori regard the ruru as a sort of guardian spirit. We must hope that Bree's tattoo will protect her until you can return her little companion to her.

"We fly to Queenstown tomorrow," I said. "If Bree's not there, I will definitely release a few pent-up emotions."

It will do your soul good. In the meantime, get some sleep. Flying out of the Wellington airport is considered by some to be one of life's greatest thrills!

I reread Aunt Dimity's final sentence warily as her words faded from the page, then closed the journal and placed it on the table.

"Call me a wimp," I muttered to Reginald, "but the prospect of another thrilling flight doesn't fill me with undiluted joy."

I patted his head and Ruru's, turned out the light, and fell into an uneasy sleep, wondering what fresh terrors New Zealand had in store for me.

We took off sideways. I didn't know that a plane *could* take off sideways until we finished zigzagging down the runway and became airborne, by which time I'd lost the will to live.

"Now you know why it's called Windy Wellington," Cameron said, with a certifiably insane shout of laughter. "The North Island and the South Island are separated by the Cook Strait, which acts as a wind tunnel. The weather was unusually placid yesterday, but it's business as usual today."

"Lucky me," I croaked. For some reason, my mouth had gone dry.

"Should be smooth sailing from here on in," he assured me. "Nothing but blue skies ahead."

"And blue sea below," I said, peering at the strait's white-capped, roiling waves. "Is your airplane equipped with life vests?"

"Relax, Lori," said Cameron. "The best is yet to come."

"Define what you mean by 'the best,'" I said, eyeing him suspiciously.

"Four million people live in New Zealand," he said. "Only one million live on the South Island. It's uncrowded, unspoiled, and incredible. You'll see."

I did see. I saw the Southern Alps, a majestic spine of razor-edged mountains that ran the entire length of the South Island. I caught glimpses of tarns, waterfalls, glaciers, and the glistening pinnacle of Mount Aspiring. I saw Aoraki/Mount Cook, New Zealand's tall-est mountain, where Sir Edmund Hillary honed his climbing skills before tackling Everest. I saw clouds reflected with surreal preci-sion in the mirrorlike surface of Lake Tekapo, and gazed in awe at the sheer-walled fjord called Milford Sound, a haven for penguins, seals, dolphins, and boatloads of tourists. I saw enough breath-taking beauty to make me wish with all my heart for a chance to see more.

My head was so full of spectacular images that I thought it would burst when the snowcapped, serried peaks of the Remark-ables range came into view, rising like white flames above the azure waters of Lake Wakatipu. Queenstown hugged the lake's shore, clung to the foothills surrounding it, and spilled into adjoining valleys, but the city was dwarfed by the absurdly lovely landscape that surrounded it.

Our touchdown on the grass strip at the Queenstown Airport was as humdrum as our takeoff had been thrilling. If I was a bit wobbly when I climbed out of the plane, it was only because I'd absorbed a surfeit of unforgettable sights.

"Well?" said Cameron, handing over my duffel bag. "What's the verdict?"

"I don't know what to say," I said, gazing wide-eyed at the Remarkables. "The North Island was pretty amazing, but the South Island . . ." I shook my head. "Words fail me."

"Me, too," he said, with a satisfied smile. "Let's pick up the car. We're renting one this time."

"Don't you have any friends in Queenstown?" I inquired, walking with him toward the terminal.

"I have quite a few friends in Queenstown," he replied, "but at the moment they have no vehicles to spare."

The gray Subaru Outback Cameron had rented was spotlessly clean and refreshingly free of animal odors. I settled happily into the passenger's seat, contemplating the manifold pleasures of riding in a car that smelled like . . . a car.

"How on earth did Bree's beat-up old Ford make it over those mountain ranges?" I asked as we pulled away from the airport.

"She probably drove down the east coast," Cameron replied. "It's not quite as rugged as the west. You and I took the scenic route."

"We certainly did," I agreed. "What route will we take now?"

"We'll check in to our hotel and ask the concierge for directions to Angelo's Café," he said. "The café's manager claimed that he'd seen Bree around town. He may be able to give us a lead."

"I won't complain if he gives us a plateful of chicken wings as well," I said. "Scenic routes make me hungry."

My balcony in the thoroughly modern Novotel Hotel was so close to Lake Wakatipu that I could hear ducks quacking as they landed on the water. It provided a tranquil alternative to the vibrant city center.

Queenstown seemed bent on retaining its status as New Zealand's adventure capital. As we'd driven down bustling Shotover Street on our way to the hotel, I'd spotted signs touting bungee jumping, jet boating, horse trekking, kayaking, skydiving, downhill skiing, white-water rafting, hot air ballooning, canyoning, snowboarding, parasailing, helicopter flights, and four-wheel-drive tours. After scanning the eager faces of the town's youthful population, I could only hope that there was a good hospital nearby, staffed with a talented team of orthopedic surgeons.

Since Cameron wasn't a big fan of Buffalo chicken wings—a confession I vowed never to share with the Velesuonnos—we had a light and probably much healthier lunch at the Halo Café, which was conveniently located across the street from the hotel. From there we followed the concierge's directions to an alley called Searle Lane, where we found Angelo's Café. The place was so busy I knew the wing king would forgive us for dining elsewhere.

I waited outside while Cameron charmed his way through a throng of chattering customers to the front counter. A moment later, he returned to the alleyway accompanied by Andrew Rosen, the café's manager.

Andrew Rosen was a rotund gentleman with wiry gray hair, a neatly trimmed gray beard, and a wonderful smile. He, unlike his boss, was a laid-back and soft-spoken Kiwi. He called a friendly hello to numerous passersby and took our interrogation in stride.

"Yes, that's right, I gave Angelo a call after I read the girl's application," he told us, wiping his hands on his apron. "I'd never seen him used as a reference before, so it caught my attention."

"We're glad it did," I said, "because we need to find this girl."

"Too bad I didn't hire her on the spot," he said ruefully. "If I had, your search would be over."

We stood aside as an attractive family of four exited the café. The husband and wife stopped briefly to chat with Andrew and each of the bright-eyed little girls gave him a hug before departing.

"Angelo's tenants," he said, by way of explanation.

"The Robbins?" I said, flabbergasted.

"Yes," said Andrew, looking mildly amused. "I take it that Angelo mentioned them to you?"

"He asked me to say g'day to the Robbins family for him and Renee," I answered distractedly, watching the family turn onto the street at the end of Searle Lane.

"I'll give them the message," Andrew assured me. "The Robbins eat here at least twice a week. Rhonda and Lee—the mum and dad—aren't too keen on fried food, but Sharni and Keira have fallen in love with our wings."

"I can't believe we actually ran into them," I said, shaking my head.

"Queenstown is like that," he said. "Everyone gravitates to the city center, either for work or for play. It's a lucky thing, too, because you won't have far to go to find the girl you're looking for."

"Y-you know where she is?" I stuttered, blinking in disbelief.

"I know where she went after she left here," he said. "She got a job at the Southern Lakes Gallery. It's on Beach Street, a ten-minute stroll from here. Holly Mortensen is the owner. I believe she opened a new exhibit today. Tell her I said hello, will you?"

"Andrew," I cried, flinging my arms around his neck and planting a kiss on his bearded cheek, "I would walk through fire for you."

Sixteen

ameron and I turned the ten-minute stroll into a five-minute dash. As we raced nimbly around knots of ambling shoppers, I tried not to get overexcited. Our quarry had eluded us too often for me to believe that she might, at last, be within reach.

We skidded to a halt in front of the Southern Lakes Gallery, paused briefly to catch our breath, and went inside. The gallery's bare hardwood floor and stark white walls provided an uncluttered background for a collection of abstract oil paintings. Several dozen wine glasses sat, apparently untouched, on an oak refectory table to the left of the entrance, behind a tasteful sign announcing the opening of an exhibit of works by Axel Turke, a name I did not recognize.

A weedy, dark-haired, bespectacled young man sat hunched over the keys of a baby grand piano at the far end of the long, narrow room, playing a haunting tune that was, like the painter's name, unfamiliar to me. The pianist was the only person present in the gallery, apart from me and Cameron, and he was so absorbed in his music that he didn't look up when we entered.

"Axel Turke doesn't seem to be too popular," Cameron murmured.

"Maybe we missed the rush," I murmured back. I cleared my throat to catch the pianist's attention. When he failed to respond, I called out, "Excuse me? Can you help us?"

The pianist glanced at us but continued to play as he shouted, "Holly! You're wanted!"

A door in the back wall opened and the gallery's owner appeared. I hadn't seen anyone like her since I'd arrived in New Zealand. She wore her bleached blond hair in a sleek bob and she was fully made up—eyeliner, mascara, red lipstick, the works. A sleeveless, wheat-colored sheath dress flattered her svelte figure, gold bangles drew attention to her manicured hands, and a pair of ivory sandals with stiletto heels revealed a meticulous pedicure. Queenstown's college-age mob might bum around in ripped T-shirts and cargo shorts, but Holly Mortensen was as chic as her gallery.

"Simon?" she said into thin air. "Wine, please."

She favored us with a slightly predatory smile as she walked toward us, her stilettos rat-a-tatting on the hardwood floor. Behind her, a tall, round-shouldered man emerged from the doorway and hastened after her. He had a long, lugubrious face and his blond hair was so sparse that at first sight he appeared to be bald. He was dressed like a waiter, in a white shirt and black trousers, and he carried a round wooden tray laden with three wine bottles. Although the bottles had been opened, they were still full. I glanced at the untouched wine glasses and wondered if *anyone* had attended the exhibit's opening.

"How good of you to come," said Holly, shaking hands with each of us in turn. "I hope you're as excited by Axel's work as we are. He's a local artist—a local *genius,* I should say—and we're proud to be the first to present his visionary paintings to the public."

"I, um . . ." I faltered, looking askance at the canvases. I didn't want to rain on Holly's parade, but I didn't care for oil paintings, and abstracts simply weren't my cup of tea.

"I understand," she said with a fatalistic sigh. "You prefer pretty watercolors of country cottages with roses round the doors."

"Well," I said, a touch defensively, "yes, I do."

"And you?" said Holly, turning her sights on Cameron.

"Equestrian portraits," he replied.

"Never mind." Holly folded her slender arms and shrugged resignedly. "I promised Axel's mother that I'd stage a show for him, but she seems to be his only fan." She crooked a finger at the long-faced man, who'd placed his tray on the oak table. "Simon? We're in need of refreshment."

Simon poured a generous splash of red wine into a glass, presented it to Holly, and waited at her elbow for further instructions.

"May I offer you a drink?" Holly asked me and Cameron. "We have Mount Difficulty pinot noir, pinot gris, and dry Riesling. I suggest that you taste all three. The vineyard's in Central Otago—one of our finest wine-growing regions—and the wine is simply superb."

"To tell you the truth," I said, "my friend and I didn't come here to look at Axel's artwork *or* to sample your wine. We're trying to locate someone, and Andrew Rosen told us that she works for you."

"She?" said Holly, with a slight frown. "Do you mean Bree Pym?"

"Yes," I said, nodding vigorously. "We're looking for Bree Pym."

"I'm afraid she's not here," said Holly.

"Did you fire her?" I asked, scanning the gallery for signs of breakage.

"No," said Holly, looking startled.

"Did she quit?" Cameron asked.

"*No,*" Holly replied sharply, "and I hope she won't. She's an excellent assistant. She has an eye for art and a head for numbers. It's a rare combination. I wish she didn't have quite so many piercings, but—"

"She's *pierced* herself?" I said, aghast.

"Nose ring, eyebrow stud, and a half dozen holes in each ear," said Holly. "She can hide her tattoos with long sleeves, but the piercings are on permanent display. Her appearance puts off some of my more refined customers, so I've asked her to stay in back when they're around. She doesn't mind. She understands marketing."

"If Bree's such a treasure," I snapped, "why isn't she here?"

Holly eyed me speculatively as she sipped her wine. After a moment's silence, she asked, "Who *are* you?"

It suddenly dawned on me that neither Cameron nor I had introduced ourselves. From Holly's point of view it must have looked as though a pair of teetotaling philistines had burst into her gallery, demanding to know the whereabouts of one of her best employees. Had I been in her stylish shoes, I, too, would have asked a few questions.

"Forgive me," I said. "Please allow me to explain. . . ."

By the time I finished describing my mission, Holly had polished off her first glass of wine and started in on a second; Simon had carried the bottle of pinot noir closer to her, to facilitate refills; and the pianist had paused long enough to stretch his fingers before launching into another haunting piece.

"So you see," I concluded, "my friend and I would be *endlessly* grateful to you if you'd tell us where we might find Bree Pym."

"I would if I could, but I can't," said Holly. "Sunday is her day off."

"It's Sunday?" I said, taken aback. "I had no idea. . . . I guess I've lost track of time."

"You've had other things on your mind," Holly said generously. "I honestly don't know what Bree does on her days off, but Gary might. He and Bree have become great friends. She admires his music."

As she turned to speak to the pianist, the floor jerked sideways, the wine bottles toppled over, and the whole building seemed to emit a low-pitched rumble. Cameron seized me by the shoulders and shoved me under the oak table, where Holly and Simon had already taken refuge. He dove in after me and the four of us huddled together while the floor shook, the glasses rattled, and the bottles rolled.

"Earthquake," Cameron said in my ear.

"Are you kidding me?" I said, my hands splayed against the twitching floor. *"Are you kidding me?"*

"First one?" Holly asked conversationally.

"Uh-huh," I replied, watching the paintings sway back and forth on the walls.

"It'll soon be over," said Cameron.

I felt two more big jolts and I don't know how many smaller ones before the shaking ceased. I started to crawl out from under the table, but Cameron and Simon hauled me back.

"Aftershocks," said Holly. "You might want to stay put for a bit." She cocked her head toward Simon, who was clutching the bottle of pinot noir as though his life, or possibly his job, depended on it. "Glass of wine?"

"No thank you," I said tersely.

I waited for the others to give the all-clear, then followed their example and got to my feet. Cameron looked supremely unconcerned, Simon hadn't spilled a drop of wine, and Holly hadn't even smeared her lipstick. The pianist straightened his sheet music and resumed playing, as though nothing out of the ordinary had happened.

"What a waste," Holly said, surveying the puddles of pinot gris and dry Riesling spreading from the toppled bottles. "Clear it up, will you, Simon? I'll see to the pictures."

"What's *wrong* with you people?" I exploded, looking from one calm face to the next. "How can you be so . . . *blasé*? We've just survived an *earthquake*."

Simon gave me a vaguely puzzled glance, then retreated to the back room. Holly patted me on the shoulder.

"Don't upset yourself, Lori," she said. "Earthquakes are a part of life in New Zealand. The whole country's riddled with fault lines."

"Gosh, thanks," I said bleakly. "I feel much better now."

"And for that reason," Cameron continued, "we have extremely strict building codes. Look around you, Lori. The roof hasn't caved in. The walls haven't collapsed. I think I see a small crack in the front window, but it hasn't shattered. Nothing will protect us from a monster quake, but we've learned how to live with the everyday ones."

"It's a small price to pay," said Holly, "for living in God's own country."

The knowing look she exchanged with Cameron reminded me that I was a stranger in a strange land, yet I had an inkling of what had passed between them. New Zealand might not be the safest place to live, I thought, but they wouldn't trade its astonishing beauty for all the safety in the world.

Simon returned with a mop and a bucket, breaking the spell that had fallen over the gallery.

"About Bree," Cameron prompted.

"Ah, yes," said Holly. "I was about to introduce you to Gary before we were so rudely interrupted. Gary Whiterider," she added, as we approached the dark-haired pianist. "Remember his name. Gary doesn't simply play the piano. He's a composer as well, and I believe he'll be famous one day."

"If he's playing his own compositions, I believe it, too," I said. "They're gorgeous."

Holly had to rap her knuckles on the grand piano's lid to rouse Gary Whiterider from his musical trance. He blinked up at us owlishly, then folded his hands in his lap.

"Sorry," he said with a sheepish grin. "I get carried away when I'm working on a new piece."

"I don't blame you," I told him. "Your music carries me away, too."

"Thanks," he said, looking embarrassed but gratified by the compliment.

"Gary," said Holly, "these people need to speak with Bree Pym. Do you know where she is?"

"I agreed to meet her in the Queenstown Gardens after I finished here," he said. "I expect you'll find her near the Scott Memorial."

"The Scout Memorial?" I said.

"Scott," Holly corrected me. "Captain Robert Falcon Scott, to be precise—the Antarctic explorer. The memorial was erected as a tribute to him and to the men who died with him on their way back from the South Pole. It's quite touching, really. The inscription runs, in part: 'They rest in the great white silence, wrapped in the winding sheets of the eternal snows.'"

"Wasn't Scott English?" I asked.

"He was," said Holly, "but so was New Zealand, in those days. Captain Scott and his men were tragic heroes of the British Empire. Their deaths were mourned worldwide." She frowned perplexedly at Gary. "It's a gloomy spot for a tryst, I would have thought."

Gary's face turned beet-red.

"Bree and I aren't . . . We're not . . . I'm buying her *car* from her," he managed after a few false starts. "Meeting at the Scott Memorial wasn't *my* idea. It was *hers*."

If I could have chosen a place for Bree to linger, it wouldn't have been near a monument commemorating the tragic deaths of a doomed party of Antarctic explorers. I glanced at Cameron, who nodded.

"Hate to chat and run," he said briskly, "but Lori and I must be on our way."

"Thank you very much, Gary," I said. "If you ever make a CD, I'll buy a boxful."

We said good-bye to Holly, Gary, and silent Simon, left the Southern Lakes Gallery, and turned toward Marine Parade, a lakefront boulevard that would, according to Cameron, take us directly to the Queenstown Gardens.

"They're next door to our hotel," he informed me.

"You mean we're running in circles?" I said. "Why am I not surprised?"

Cameron laughed and picked up his pace, and I increased mine as well. In a few short minutes, I told myself, our persistence would finally pay off.

Seventeen

We jogged past a waterfront park, a jet-boat dock, and a bronze statue of a bearded man who appeared to be petting a remarkably woolly ram. We ran past our hotel, a family of ducks patrolling a gravelly beach, and a playfully decorated octagonal restaurant that, Cameron explained on the fly, had originally been a bathhouse built to celebrate the coronation of King George V. We crossed a gurgling brook on a wooden footbridge to enter the Queenstown Gardens, but when we reached the first park bench, Cameron came to a sudden halt.

"What are you doing?" I asked, swinging around to face him.

"I'll wait for you here," he said. "It'll be easier on Bree if you approach her alone. One person will be less alarming than two, and a woman will be less threatening than a man. Besides, it's *your* mission. You should be the one to accomplish it."

"But you've been with me every step of the way," I protested. "It won't feel right to reach the end of the journey without you."

"Only one part of the journey will be over," said Cameron. "I'll be around for the rest of it." He sat on the bench and pointed to his right. "Follow the path. The Scott Memorial is a big boulder surrounded by flower beds and a short hedge. The path will lead you to it."

Cameron had clearly made up his mind, so there was no point in arguing with him. I nodded reluctantly and took off down the path, feeling slightly dejected and a tiny bit fearful. What would I do if Bree flew into a rage? I wondered. Fend her off with my day pack? Reginald and Ruru wouldn't make much of an impact, but the biscuit tin would pack a good punch. I slipped the day pack from my shoulders and held it by its straps in one hand, the better to swing it with.

If I hadn't been so preoccupied with defensive measures, I would have enjoyed my solitary stroll. The weather was splendid and the gardens weren't devoted exclusively to flowers. The path meandered past a lily pad–laden pond, a croquet lawn, a bowling green, and a set of tennis courts. It wound its way through trees adorned with glorious spring blossoms to a formal rose garden, which hadn't yet come into bloom. And each time I remembered to look up, there was Lake Wakatipu, glinting through the greenery.

Beyond the rose garden sat an enormous gray granite boulder inset with a pair of marble plaques. Above the plaques, five white marble stars formed a constellation that had guided explorers for centuries. I gazed at the stars and realized, with a warm rush of affection, that Cameron had kept the promise he'd made to me in Ohakune. I'd finally seen the Southern Cross.

The somber purple flowers surrounding the boulder were enclosed by a knee-high hedge interspersed with short granite columns. A girl sat on the grass with her back to one of the columns, reading a ragged paperback copy of *The Return of the King,* the third book in Tolkien's trilogy. She wore blue jeans, sneakers, and a black tank top. A greenstone pendant carved in the shape of a koru—an opening fern frond—hung around her neck. A dark-blue hooded sweatshirt and a canvas book bag lay by her side.

I recognized her immediately. The spiky hair, the tattoos, and the piercings did nothing to diminish Bree's dark beauty. Angelo had been right, I thought. A girl like that could shave her head and still be a knockout.

"Excuse me," I said quietly. I didn't want to startle her.

Bree raised her heart-shaped face. Her slight build made her look younger than eighteen, but when I gazed into her liquid brown eyes I saw someone who had forgotten, or who had never known, how to be young.

"I'm sorry to interrupt your reading," I said.

"No worries." She sat up and closed the book. "Do you want to take a picture of the memorial? I'll get out of your way."

"I'm not interested in the memorial," I said, motioning for her to remain seated. "My name is Lori Shepherd and I came here to speak with you."

Bree's eyes narrowed slightly, and I tightened my grip on my day pack, but to my relief she seemed curious rather than hostile.

"How did you know I'd be here?" she asked.

"I've been to the Southern Lakes Gallery," I replied. "Gary White-rider told me where to find you."

"Are you an American?" she asked.

"Yes," I said, "but I live in England."

Bree slipped the book into her bag and leaned back against the granite column. "Why would an American living in England want to speak with me?"

"It's a long story," I said, "but there are a few things you need to know before I tell it." I dropped my day pack on the ground and sat beside it, facing her. "I visited your flat in Auckland a few days ago. While I was there, a nurse from North Shore Hospital stopped by. She was the nurse who looked after your father while he was in the critical care unit."

"Is he dead?" she asked, without a flicker of emotion.

I nodded, murmuring, "I'm sorry."

Bree sighed softly and bowed her head. "Did he ask for me before he died?"

"Yes," I said. "The nurse told me that he asked for you repeatedly. When it became apparent that you weren't going to show up, he asked her to give you a message. He wanted you to know that he was sorry."

"Again," Bree murmured with a bitter laugh.

"The nurse would appreciate it if you'd call her as soon as possible," I continued. "She has your father's personal effects and she needs to know what you want to do with his . . . remains." I took Bridgette Burkhoffer's business card from my pack and handed it to Bree. "You can use my cell phone to call her, if you like."

Bree studied the card, then shook her head.

"I can't afford a funeral," she said.

"Not a problem," I told her. "I'll cover the expenses."

Bree frowned at me. "Why would you pay for my father's funeral?"

"I'm a friend of the family," I said.

"What kind of friend?" she asked, her face hardening.

Her reaction brought to mind Amanda's admission that Ed hadn't been the most faithful of husbands. I quickly raised a pacifying hand.

"Not *that* kind," I assured her. "I never met your father. I wasn't even sure where New Zealand *was* until a few days ago, but I've seen an awful lot of it since then. I've been chasing you all over the place. I've followed you from Auckland to the Hokianga and from Ohakune to Wellington. I've spoken with your horrible landlady and your father's nurse. I've spent time with Amanda and Daniel, Angelo and Renee, Kitta and Kati, and Holly and Gary, among others, because I had to find out where you were. I said it was a long story, but I should have called it an epic *saga*. And now here I am, sitting in the Queenstown Gardens, face-to-face with you at last. I don't think I would have gone to all of that trouble if I were one of your father's, um, *acquaintances*."

"Why *did* you go to all of that trouble?" Bree asked, looking understandably bewildered.

"For one thing, I had to return *this* to you." I pulled Ruru out of my pack, smoothed his mottled wings, and deposited him gently in Bree's hands. "Try not to lose him again, okay?"

"Where did you find him?" asked Bree, peering dazedly at the bedraggled little owl.

"You left him behind when you sneaked out of the Velesuonnos' condo," I said, "which, by the way, was a pretty thoughtless thing to do."

"How do you know—"

"I'm sure you were embarrassed about the hissy fit you threw at the tattoo parlor," I interrupted, "but you shouldn't have disappeared like a thief in the night. Kati and Kitta deserved a more polite farewell. As a matter of fact, so did Roger, but we did what we could to make it up to him. My friend Cameron paid for the glasses and the lamp, which reminds me," I went on, struck by a sudden thought, "I have to pay him back."

"Cameron?" said Bree. "Who's Cameron?"

"He's my native guide," I explained. "Without his help, and his airplane, and his encyclopedic knowledge of your country, I never would have found you."

"Why did you *want* to find me?" Bree demanded, her dark eyes flashing. *"Why have you been following me?"*

"Because I'm doing a favor for two very dear old ladies," I answered calmly. "Ruth and Louise Pym are my friends as well as my neighbors. They also happen to be your great-grandaunts."

Bree's mouth fell open and the color drained from her face. She stared at me in dumbfounded disbelief, then whispered, "The English aunts? It's not possible. They must be dead by now."

"They're not. They're just getting on in years. Would you like a biscuit?" I asked, taking Donna's chintz-patterned tin out of my pack. "Sugar is good for shock and you look as though you're about to pass out."

"I feel as if I've seen a ghost," Bree said faintly.

"I know the feeling," I told her, with complete sincerity, "but Ruth and Louise aren't ghosts. They may not be in the best of health, but they're still alive. At least they were alive when I spoke with my husband last night. The situation may have changed since then, though I hope it hasn't." I opened the tin and held it out to Bree. "Help yourself. Something tells me that we'll be here for a while."

Bree munched on Anzac biscuits and listened almost without blinking while I repeated everything Fortescue Makepeace and Aunt Dimity had told me about Aubrey Jeremiah Pym, Sr., and his identical twin sisters. By the time I finished, the sky had turned from blue to steely gray and a brisk wind had begun to whip the treetops. Bree had donned her hooded sweatshirt midway through my monologue and I'd slipped into my rain jacket.

"Ruth and Louise didn't know your branch of the family existed until they found the letter in their mother's trunk," I concluded. "They asked me to come to New Zealand because they wanted to reach out to their nephew—your grandfather—before it was too late."

"But Granddad was dead," Bree said, "and my father was dead. So you came to find me."

"You're Ruth's and Louise's only surviving relative," I said, reaching into my day pack for the letter Bill had e-mailed to Donna

Mackenzie. "Look, Bree, I realize that the situation may seem improbable, but—"

"It doesn't seem improbable to me," she broke in. "Ruth and Louise aren't the only members of my family who've been kept in the dark. I didn't know a thing about my great-grandfather until I read Granddad's obituary. He wrote it himself." Her brow furrowed as she rummaged through her book bag. "He must have written it during the day, while I was at school."

I left the letter in the day pack and watched her intently, wondering what she wanted to show me. Her search produced a folded newspaper clipping. When she unfolded the clipping, I saw that it was the same size as the blank spot I'd noticed on the corkboard in her bedroom and that it had a telltale pinhole in each corner. A. J. had apparently written a lengthy account of his life because the typeface was miniscule.

I expected Bree to pass the clipping to me, but she kept hold of it.

"Tell me about my great-grandaunts," she said, without preamble. "What did they do for a living before they retired?"

"I don't think they did anything for a living," I replied readily. It seemed only natural that Bree should be curious about her newly discovered relatives. "They're magnificent gardeners and accomplished seamstresses and they're on the flower-arranging rota at the local church, but as far as I know, neither one of them has ever held a paying job."

"Have they ever had any trouble making ends meet?" Bree asked.

"No," I said. "And believe me, if they had, I would have heard about it. News like that gets around faster than fleas in Finch." I smiled. "You don't have to be concerned about them, Bree. Ruth and Louise live quite comfortably."

"My great-grandaunts have never worked a day in their lives, yet they live quite comfortably." Bree raised her pierced eyebrow. "Haven't you ever wondered how they pay for their comforts?"

I shrugged. "I assumed that their father—"

"Their father was a village parson," Bree interrupted impatiently. "Even if he'd scrimped and saved, he couldn't have left them enough money to enable them to live in comfort for the rest of their lives."

"I suppose not," I acknowledged equably. "I'm sorry, but I can't answer your question, Bree. I don't know anything about your great-grandaunts' financial affairs."

"Granddad did." She glanced down at the newspaper clipping, then stowed it and Ruru in her bag. "Granddad wrote about the English aunts in his obituary."

"What did he write?" I asked.

Once Bree started speaking the words came tumbling out, as if she'd longed to confide in someone but had known full well that no one would believe or understand her. The intensity of her loneliness came home to me as I realized that there were only two people in her entire country to whom her story would make sense. One was the American woman who sat in front of her, and the other was sitting on a park bench, waiting for me.

"My great-grandfather, Aubrey Jeremiah Pym, Senior, was for a short time one of the wealthiest men in New Zealand," she began. "He got rich by marrying an heiress named Stella McConchie."

In my mind's eye I saw the silver-framed wedding portrait Cameron and I had discovered on the mantelshelf in A. J.'s filthy flat. Cameron had said at the time that it looked as though Aubrey had married money, and Bree had confirmed his guess. Aubrey, it seemed, had used his charm and his dashing good looks to jump to the top of the social ladder in his adopted country.

"When he took control of Stella's money," Bree was saying, "the first thing he did was to set up a trust fund for the sisters he'd left behind in England. He tied it up in miles of red tape because he didn't want his father to touch a penny of it. He'd never gotten on well with his father."

I leaned forward, intrigued. It had never occurred to me that the family's black sheep, an unrepentant scoundrel who'd committed every sin short of cold-blooded murder, would behave so magnanimously.

"Aubrey didn't get on well with the McConchie family, either," Bree went on. "They didn't approve of him, so when Stella died in childbirth and Aubrey reverted to his bad old habits, they turned their backs on him and his newborn son. Aubrey drank and gambled his way through the rest of his fortune in less than a year. His sisters' money was safe, though. Aubrey had tied it up so tightly that not even he could touch it. When he died in the Great War, therefore, his penniless son was put into an orphanage."

I thought of the mustachioed man holding the lace-bedecked baby in the arched entryway of ChristChurch Cathedral, and bowed my head. Aubrey had gone from rags to riches in five short years, but while he'd enjoyed the riches, his son had been left nothing but rags.

"Granddad beat the odds," said Bree, with a wan smile. "He had a rough start at the orphanage, but he made a success of his life. Then he and Gran had Ed. I don't know what they did to deserve a son like Ed, but it must have been terrible because Ed grew up to be a worthless piece of . . . tripe."

She huddled more deeply into her sweatshirt, but the chill she felt seemed to come from within, not from the swirling breezes. When I suggested that we move indoors she didn't seem to hear me.

"Ed broke his parents' hearts," she went on. "He drank, he stole, he lied, and he manipulated everyone who tried to help him. His mum and dad ordered him to leave home on his eighteenth birthday because they couldn't stand the chaos anymore. When Amanda showed up years later with their granddaughter in tow, they felt as if they'd been given a second chance at parenthood. They took the child in and showered her with the love Ed had squandered. Granddad set aside money for her education and Gran told her that she had a bright future ahead of her."

Bree stared at the ground with unfocused eyes, lost in memories. Then her lips tightened.

"But Ed came back," she said. "My grandparents believed him when he promised to clean up his act. The prodigal son had returned and they rejoiced. But his saintly phase didn't last."

"He reverted to his bad old habits," I murmured.

"He drove Gran to an early grave," said Bree. "And Granddad and I became his prisoners. I was too young to throw him out and Granddad was too old, so he took over. He sold Gran's jewelry to pay off his gambling debts. He forced Granddad to cash in his investments and to sell the furniture, the house, the cars." Bree lifted her chin. "But Granddad refused to touch the money he'd set aside for me. Ed threatened to kill him for it, but Granddad said he'd rather die than to see my future thrown away at the track."

"Why didn't your grandfather report Ed to the police?" I asked.

"I wouldn't let him," she replied, as if she were stating the obvious. "My grandparents had never adopted me formally, and I was still underage. If the police had gotten involved, I might have been put into care and there would have been no one to look after Granddad."

The wind had let up, but the temperature had taken a nosedive. I was certain that Bree was as cold and stiff as I was, but she didn't show it. She sat with her back to the granite column and her arms wrapped around her knees, occasionally meeting my eyes, but staring mostly at the ground.

"Eventually," she said, "we had nothing to live on but Granddad's pension, my education fund, and the money Ed brought in when he felt like working. We should have found a cheaper flat in another part of the city, but Granddad wanted me to go to a good school, so we stayed in Takapuna. I left the day after I buried him."

"And went looking for your mother," I said.

"I thought she might . . ." Bree's face crumpled, but she quickly mastered her emotions. "But it was no good. Every time Amanda looked at me, she thought of Ed. I could see it in her eyes."

"She called you her *taonga*," I murmured. "Her treasure."

"Some treasures are cursed," Bree said harshly. "So I moved on."

"Your mother told me that Ed cursed the English aunts," I said.

"He did," said Bree. "He blamed them for ruining his life. If the English aunts hadn't robbed us blind, he would have been wealthy, famous, influential. He kept the silver picture frames as proof of our family's lost riches. I didn't know what he was talking about until I read Granddad's obituary."

"How did Ed find out about the English aunts?" I asked.

"Granddad must have mentioned them somewhere along the line," said Bree, "but he never mentioned them to me." She peered puzzledly into the middle distance. "Maybe he thought I would resent them."

"Do you?" I asked.

"No." Bree's mouth twisted in a humorless smile. "Money didn't make Granddad a good man, and the lack of it didn't turn Ed into a monster. If Ed had inherited a million dollars, he would have blown it all on booze and bets. I'm glad the money went to two women who like flowers."

"I think they'd like you, too," I said.

"I doubt it," said Bree, wrapping her arms more tightly around her knees. "Ex-cons have trouble adjusting to life after prison. I disappointed my teachers by not going on to university. I haven't been able to hold on to a job since I left Takapuna. I attacked Roger for no good reason, and I expect I'll do the same to Holly. I don't know how to behave around normal people." She pressed her hands to her eyes. "I've given up hope of learning."

"No you haven't," I said.

She lowered her hands and regarded me dubiously.

"You may not be aware of it," I said, "but you've surrounded yourself with hope." I pointed at her book bag. "Tolkien threaded strands of hope through all of his stories." I motioned toward her neck. "The pendant you're wearing is a koru, a symbol of new life and new beginnings." I jutted my chin toward the Scott Memorial. "You didn't come here to dwell on death. You're sitting with your back to the boulder, facing trees arrayed in the rainbow colors of spring." I fixed her with a level gaze. "I don't deny that you've been through hell, Bree, but it's not in your nature to give in to despair. Your spirit is too strong."

"And look where my strength has gotten me," she retorted. "No car, no home, no friends, and no future. I don't know where to go from here."

"If I might make a suggestion?" I said, with a tentative smile.

"You may be impervious to the cold, but my bum is numb and I'm starving. Why don't we pick up Cameron and have a hot meal, preferably in front of a roaring fire? It's getting dark, anyway, so unless you have a flashlight, you won't be able to read the letter."

"What letter?" she asked.

"Didn't I tell you about your great-grandaunts' letter?" I hit myself in the forehead. "My brain must be frostbitten. Let's go somewhere warm before I lose consciousness. You can read the letter there."

Bree kept still for a moment, curled in upon herself like a frightened child. She closed her eyes and released an exhausted sigh, then unfolded like an opening fern frond, got to her feet, and walked with me through the blossoming trees to Cameron.

Eighteen

We ate at the Bathhouse Restaurant because it was close at hand, open on Sunday evening, and heated. The elegant decor, the excellent service, the creative menu, and the unmatched views of Lake Wakatipu were pleasant bonuses. Had we been in England, or even the United States, I might have hesitated to enter such a sophisticated establishment in grass-stained trousers and a wrinkled rain jacket, but New Zealand's restaurateurs had a refreshing come-as-you-are attitude toward attire that put me at ease.

Another advantage to the Coronation Bathhouse was that it, unlike many eateries in youth-oriented Queenstown, did not feature a live band. The muted atmosphere allowed Bree to concentrate on her great-grandaunts' letter while Cameron and I ordered a sumptuous dinner for our party of three.

When she finished reading the letter, Bree asked to borrow my cell phone and stepped away from the table to make a call. She returned a short time later, handed the phone back to me, and maintained a preoccupied silence throughout the meal. How she could refrain from cooing ecstatically over the braised pork dumplings, the kumara and feta gnocchi, and the manuka honey sorbet was beyond me, but she didn't make a sound until the Valrhona chocolate cake arrived at our table.

"The lawyer didn't tell them that the money came from Aubrey," she said.

"Lawyer?" I managed, through a mouthful of chocolaty goodness. I pondered her words for a moment, then asked, "Are you referring to Fortescue Makepeace?"

She nodded. "Mr. Makepeace's grandfather agreed never to mention Aubrey's name again after Aubrey was disinherited, so he couldn't tell Ruth and Louise about the trust fund Aubrey set up for them. His son and his grandson were bound by the same agreement. The Fortescues managed the fund for nearly a century without ever telling Ruth and Louise where the money came from. My great-grandaunts believed all along that their father had made canny investments for them." She gave a shaky laugh. "How could anyone be so naive?"

"Don't judge them by today's standards," Cameron advised. "When Ruth and Louise were growing up, women weren't expected to deal with financial matters. Money was a vulgar subject best left to the menfolk."

"It sounds as if they know about the trust fund now," I said. "What happened? Did Fortescue Makepeace break his vow of silence and tell them the truth?"

"No," said Bree. "He told the truth to someone named Nell Harris, who told it to Ruth and Louise."

"Why did he spill the beans to Nell?" I asked.

"Because she helped Ruth and Louise to draft a new will." Bree gazed at me wonderingly. "My great-grandaunts have left everything to me. *Everything.* Not just the income from the trust, but *everything they own*—the house and all of its contents, the land, the car—"

"I wouldn't get too jazzed about the car," I cautioned. "It might have been a top-of-the-line model when it was first produced, but it's a museum piece now." I saw that Bree was trembling and added bracingly, "Of course they're leaving everything to you. They've spent most of their lives being honorary aunts. If you hadn't come along, they would never have known what it's like to be *real* aunts. I'd say you're just about the best thing that's ever happened to them."

Bree clasped her hands together, as if to steady herself. "They want to meet me. They say there's an open-ended ticket waiting for me at the airport in Auckland."

"Excellent," I said, toasting her with a forkful of cake. "You can fly back with me."

"Lori," Cameron said oppressively, "you're forgetting that Bree has unfinished business here in New Zealand."

Bree's entire demeanor changed. The excitement drained from her face and her posture became rigid.

"I don't have to decide what to do about Ed, if that's what you mean by unfinished business," she said. "I spoke with Bridgette Burkhoffer before dinner. The hospital buried Ed two days ago. They ran out of room in the morgue, so they laid him to rest in the public cemetery. He's not my responsibility anymore."

"Will they send his personal effects to you?" Cameron asked.

"I gave Bridgette my permission to throw them into the hospital's incinerator," Bree said coldly.

Cameron looked taken aback, but I caught his eye and shook my head minutely, as a signal to leave well enough alone. If Bree had to answer one more question about her late, unlamented father, I was certain she would lose it.

"There's the apartment in Takapuna," he went on hesitantly. "The family photographs, your computer . . ."

"I don't want them," she said stiffly. "I copied the files I need and I have the photographs I want. I don't care what happens to the rest. I'm never going back to the apartment."

"Leave it to me," said Cameron with a casual wave of his hand. "I'll call the landlady in the morning and instruct her to donate the flat's contents to an op shop. Though it pains me to give her a reason to smile, I'll also let her know that she's at liberty to rent the dump to another victim—er, I mean, tenant."

"Thank you," said Bree, defrosting slightly.

"Do you have a passport?" I asked.

"Yes," she said. "I needed one for a class trip to Australia."

"Use it again for a personal trip to England," I said. "It would mean an awful lot to Ruth and Louise."

"I don't know." Bree rubbed her tattooed arms self-consciously. "What if I scare them?"

"Scare them?" I scoffed. "They're gardeners. They see a hundred things scarier than you every time they poke a spade into the dirt."

Bree managed a weak smile but she still looked doubtful.

"It must feel like everything's coming at you at a hundred miles an hour," I said gently, "and heaven knows I don't want to pressure you, but the simple truth is that Ruth and Louise may not have a whole lot of time left. They've been improving steadily for the past few days, but if you ask me, it's a temporary reprieve. No one lives forever. I think they're holding on because of you."

"No pressure there," Bree said dryly, leaning her chin on her hand.

"You don't have to move to England permanently," I said. "You can make your visit as long or as short as you like. God's own country will be waiting for you when you come back—unless it explodes, or cracks into pieces, or blows away."

Bree's smile widened infinitesimally.

"I don't want to pressure you, either," said Cameron, "but when someone pulls you from a burning building, you don't stop to say, 'Wait. This is all so sudden.' You let yourself be rescued, then say"—his eyes found mine—" 'Thank you for saving my life.' "

My jaw dropped as his words clicked into place.

"Is *that* what happened?" I cried, making heads swivel in our direction.

Cameron nodded. "An electrical short started a fire in our dorm. I tried to escape down a stairwell, but I was overcome by smoke. If Bill hadn't found me and dragged me outside, I would have burned to death."

"Who's Bill?" Bree asked.

"My husband," I said, gazing across Lake Wakatipu. "My heroic husband."

"Bree," said Cameron, "your great-grandaunts have thrown you a lifeline. I suggest you grab hold of it. Lori and I are staying at the Novotel. You can reach us there when you decide—"

"I'll come," she said abruptly.

"You will?" I said, caught off guard by her sudden change of heart.

"Yes," she said. "I'd like to thank my great-grandaunts in person. And I . . . I need to get away." After a tremulous pause, her manner became businesslike. "I'll pack tonight and call Holly in the morning. I'll be ready to leave by half past eight. Shall I meet you at the hotel?"

"Meet us for breakfast in the hotel restaurant," I told her. "You can stash your gear in my room until we check out. If for some unforeseen reason we have to stick around for an extra night, you can crash with me."

"At the Novotel?" Bree said, her eyes widening. "It'll make a change from the youth hostel."

"A nice change, I hope," I said.

"A *very* nice change," she assured me.

"I'll make the travel arrangements tonight," said Cameron with a decisive nod. "If I can snag seats for the pair of you, you'll be on your way to England tomorrow evening."

We sent Bree off in a taxi after dinner, then hurried through the frigid night air to our hotel. I gave Cameron a synopsis of Bree's story over steaming cups of hot cocoa in the bar.

"Ironic," he said when I'd finished.

"What's ironic?" I asked.

Cameron rested his folded arms on the bar. "Old man Mc-Conchie struck it rich mining gold ore. The site of his original claim is in Skipper's Canyon—only a few miles from where we're sitting."

"So Bree wound up living within a stone's throw of the source of the fortune she might have inherited," I said. "I wonder if she knows?" I sipped my hot cocoa. "Did New Zealand have its own gold rush?"

"Yes indeed," said Cameron. "If you take a jet-boat ride up the Shotover River, you'll see old mining equipment rusting away in the water. Our gold rush happened later than the one in America, but the results were the same. Boom and bust. Camp sites became towns that became ghost towns when the gold ran out. Old man McConchie was cleverer than most, though. He used his earnings to build freezer works."

"Forgive me," I said, warming my hands on my cup, "but I have no idea what freezer works are."

"New Zealand was England's abbatoir back then," Cameron explained. "Most of our sheep ended up as mutton on English dinner plates. Because of the distances involved, the meat had to be stored in refrigerated buildings and shipped in refrigerated ships. The Mc-Conchie family owned half the freezer works in the country for a time, but they went bust shortly after the Great War."

"What happened?" I asked.

"The usual," said Cameron. "When old man McConchie died, his oldest son took charge, but he wasn't as clever as his dad. He put his faith in the wrong people and the business fell apart."

"Which is unfortunate," I said, "but not terribly ironic."

"It's ironic that the McConchies looked down on Aubrey Pym as a gold digger when their own fortune was based on . . . digging gold." He looked through the bar's glass walls to Lake Wakatipu. "What a long, strange trip it's been, eh? Up and down the country, and back and forth in time. You've got to be pleased that it turned out all right in the end."

"I couldn't have done any of it without you," I said. "And Donna's biscuits."

Cameron chuckled, finished his cocoa, and got to his feet. "I'm going up. It's getting late and I promised Donna I'd call her as soon as we found Bree."

"Tell her I said hello." I turned to look up at him. "And Cameron, I want you to know——"

"See you in the morning," he interrupted. "Breakfast in the dining room at half past eight." As he walked away, he called over his shoulder, "Good night!"

"Good night," I called back, feeling mildly deflated. I'd wanted to thank him from the bottom of my heart for going out of his way to make the Pym sisters' dream come true, but it looked as though I'd have to hold on to my thanks a little longer. I shook my head, finished my own cocoa, and repaired to my room to deliver the good news to my husband.

The aftershock hit toward the end of my phone call with Bill. I thought at first that a heavy truck had driven past the hotel, then that it had been buffeted by a strong gust of wind, but as my bed continued to jiggle, I realized what was actually going on.

"Earthquake in progress," I reported dispassionately.

"Really?" said Bill. "What's it like?"

"Weird," I said, "but not terrifying. Imagine lying atop a quivering bowl of Jell-O. Something's rattling in the minibar, but nothing has fallen over. I guess that's why the lamps are attached to the bedside tables. They've been like that in every hotel room, but I didn't realize it was a safety measure. There. It's finished."

Bill gave a low whistle. "Ten points for sangfroid, Lori."

"I'm turning into a Kiwi," I said. "Nothing fazes me. Lake Wakatipu could flood its banks and I wouldn't turn a hair. It's all about living in faith, not in fear. I hope Bree can learn to live like that."

"She's taking an enormous leap of faith by coming to England with you," Bill said. "I don't know if I'd have the courage to step into the unknown at a moment's notice."

"I think you would," I said. "In fact, I'm absolutely *sure* you would. When I first met Cameron he said he'd walk through fire for you. Now I know why."

"Ah," said Bill, after a short pause. "He told you."

"I'll give you a hero's welcome when I come home," I said.

"Shouldn't it be the other way around?" he asked.

"No," I said, smiling. "We *both* know who the hero is in our house."

I held the cell phone to my heart after we said good night, then plugged it into the charger and opened the blue journal.

"Dimity?" I said. "The search is over. We found Bree."

I spent nearly an hour recapitulating the day's events and Bree's far-reaching revelations. My voice was hoarse by the time Aunt Dimity's handwriting curled across the page.

Your tale is full of twists and turns I had not anticipated, Lori. As always, truth is stranger by far than fiction. I would not have expected Aubrey to provide for his sisters.

"He may have done it in order to humiliate his father," I pointed out. "What could be more satisfying than to prove to the old man that a punk can be as charitable as a parson?"

A more charitable view would be that Aubrey was making amends as best he could. His father wouldn't have accepted a penny from him, nor would he have allowed Ruth and Louise to do so if he could have prevented it. He certainly failed to enlighten them about the source of their income. He probably considered his son's gift to be tainted.

"In a way, he was right," I said. "Don't forget that Aubrey married an heiress for her money. He was a gold digger, plain and simple."

There is nothing plain and simple about the human heart, my dear. Aubrey's initial instincts may have been mercenary, but if they'd remained so, his wife's death would not have affected him so deeply. You said that the laughter had left his eyes in the baptismal photograph. It seems to me that he was a broken man after his wife died. He may have turned to drink in order to dull the pain of losing her. It's entirely possible that he loved her as well as her money, Lori. Such things do happen.

"I'll grant you that Aubrey may have had some redeeming qualities," I conceded, "but you can't say the same thing about Edmund. Ed brutalized his parents, his wife, and his child, and thought he could make it all better by saying he was sorry."

Perhaps he was sorry. Nevertheless, I'm glad that Bree was spared the task of burying him, and that his grave is far removed from those of her grandparents. Edmund did nothing to earn his daughter's grief, and his presence will not spoil any visits she might make to the final resting place of those she loved.

"Let's hear it for overcrowded morgues," I muttered grimly.

I wonder if Bree will sleep at all tonight? She must be overwhelmed by the prospects that lie before her.

"I may be the only person in the universe who knows *exactly* how she feels," I said. "I was lost and alone once, and angry at the world. Then a fictional character from my childhood came to life and helped me to see that I wasn't lost or alone and that I didn't need to be angry. If Bree's great-grandaunts do for her what Aunt Dimity did for me, she'll be just fine."

You still have a bit of a temper.

"I guess you're not finished with me yet," I said, smiling. "And I hope you never will be."

Good night, my dearest child.

"Good night." I closed the journal, turned out the light, and snuggled under the covers, but a moment later I hopped out of bed and ran over to peer through my balcony door.

It was snowing.

Nineteen

New Zealand, it seemed, wasn't quite ready to let me go. Cameron announced at breakfast the following morning that we would have to postpone our departure for one more day because Mother Nature had sabotaged our escape route. The aftershock that had shaken my bed had also triggered a landslide that had blocked the road to the airport. The landslide wouldn't have been a big deal—the locals were adept at earthquake cleanups—if the blizzard hadn't complicated matters by dumping a foot of snow on top of it.

We were, for all intents and purposes, marooned.

Fortunately, Queenstown was a pretty fantastic place in which to spend a snow day. While Cameron went off to visit a friend, and Bree returned to the gallery to help her former boss cope with the prospect of losing her, I played tourist. I sailed across Lake Wakatipu in the TSS *Earnslaw,* a beautifully restored vintage steamship, rode an enclosed gondola to the top of Bob's Peak, and watched a profoundly adorable kiwi forage for grubs at the Kiwi Birdlife Park. I was so taken by the bird's perky personality that I bought a pair of stuffed-animal kiwis in the gift shop to bring back to Will and Rob.

After downing a burger that was nearly as big as my head at a place called Fergburger, I decided to work off the extra calories by hitting the shops. I returned to the hotel late in the afternoon, loaded down with gifts for my nearest and dearest as well as a few key items of clothing for Bree.

It had occurred to me that, despite all evidence to the contrary, it was springtime Down Under, which meant that the Northern Hemisphere was heading into winter. A hooded sweatshirt wouldn't protect Bree from the biting winds that occasionally blew through Finch, but a down jacket and a handful of merino wool sweaters would. Having spent the previous six years of my life buying clothes for two little boys, it was a pleasure to pick out items for a young woman.

Dinner became a farewell feast when Holly Mortensen, silent Simon, and Gary Whiterider joined me, Cameron, and Bree at a cheerful seafood restaurant called The Fishbone Bar & Grill. I savored every succulent bite of my steamed crayfish because I wasn't sure when I'd have another.

Bree and her friends went out for drinks after dinner, but Cameron and I elected to return to the hotel. We didn't take the most direct route, but ambled slowly along Marine Parade, past the waterfront park, the jet-boat dock, the bronze statue of the bearded man and the woolly ram. It was my way of saying a fond farewell to Queenstown.

When we reached the gravelly beach, Cameron stopped short and looked at me questioningly.

"You're awfully quiet," he said. "Something wrong?"

"No," I replied. "Everything's right. Mission accomplished. Ruth and Louise are still alive and I'm bringing their great-grandniece home to them. I couldn't be happier."

"You don't sound happy," he said.

"I am," I insisted. "I'm extremely happy. I can't wait to see Bill and Will and Rob and my father-in-law, but . . ."

"Here it comes," Cameron said under his breath.

"But I wish they were here with me," I exclaimed, sending slush flying in all directions as I stamped my foot. "And I wish we could spend the next six months exploring New Zealand. I've fallen in love with your ridiculous country, Cameron. So what if it's tried to kill me a few times? No place is perfect. I want to hike with a fantail and zoom around in a jet boat and listen to kiwis call in a kauri forest. I want to see the *real* Southern Cross and cruise Milford Sound and take a bath with Bill in Frodo's jacuzzi. I want to bake cookies with Donna and I want you to see how well my sons ride." I shook my head dismally. "And I don't think any of it will ever happen."

"It will," he said.

"I don't think so," I said, shaking the slush from my sneaker. "Donna's not the only woman with a workaholic husband. It takes ten strong men with crowbars to pry Bill away from his desk. The two of you must have had perfect attendance records at school."

"Hardly," said Cameron, laughing.

"Then you've forgotten how to play hooky," I declared. "Bill doesn't know the meaning of the word *vacation*."

"He'll learn," he said. "In fact, I can guarantee that Bill will come to New Zealand with you."

"How?" I asked.

"Follow me," he replied with an enigmatic smile.

Cameron led me to the edge of the gurgling brook we'd crossed on our way to the Queenstown Gardens. Although my feet were officially frozen, I watched curiously as he took from his pocket a small object wrapped in crinkled tissue paper.

"The friend I visited today is a greenstone artist," he said. "I asked him to make a pendant for you. He carved it in the shape of a triple twist because a triple twist symbolizes the bond of friendship. Though our paths may diverge for a time, they will inevitably come together again."

He pulled the tissue paper apart to reveal a gleaming spiral of polished greenstone strung on a thin black cord.

"Greenstone is filled with mana, or spiritual power," he went on. "If you bathe it in a running stream, it will always remember where it came from, and its mana will bring you back to Aotearoa. And next time, you'll bring your husband and your sons. I promise you, Bill won't be able to resist."

He handed the pendant to me. Tears stung my eyes as I stooped to dip it into the dancing water, straightened, and hung it around my neck.

"Cameron," I began.

"Problem solved," he said, before I could even think of the right words to say. "Time for bed, Lori. You have a long trip ahead of you tomorrow. And in case you hadn't noticed, it's *cold* out here."

He shivered theatrically, laughed, and hauled me unceremoniously up the slippery bank. New Zealanders were good at many things, I thought, but they were just plain terrible at accepting thanks.

My last day in New Zealand seemed to pass in the blink of an eye. We flew from Queenstown to Auckland, picked up the luggage I'd left at Spencer on Byron Hotel, and drove across town to the international airport. Before I knew it, I was hugging Cameron good-bye.

"It's not good-bye," he reminded me, touching my greenstone pendant. "Until we meet again, *kia ora!*"

"*Kia ora,*" I said, my voice quavering, and gave him another hug.

Neither Bree nor I talked much on the homeward journey. I was absorbed in memories of the Land of the Long White Cloud, and Bree had a veritable smorgasbord of thoughts to keep her occupied.

It was cold, dark, and rainy when we reached London, as if the monsoon that had beset me when I'd gone to see Fortescue Makepeace had continued, unabated, in my absence. I didn't have the heart to tell Bree that England's bouts of gloomy weather tended to last longer than New Zealand's. I figured that, if she stuck around for a month or so, she'd discover the unpleasant truth for herself.

Bill picked us up at Heathrow, as planned, but instead of driving us to the cottage, he took us directly to the Pym sisters' redbrick house.

"There's no time to spare," he informed us quietly. "They've taken a turn for the worse."

Bree hastened through the wrought-iron gate without pausing to survey the house, as though she didn't want us to suspect her of being more interested in her inheritance than in those who were leaving it to her. It was just as well, I told myself, because the front garden looked depressingly neglected.

Nell met us at the door. She greeted us serenely, but as she ushered us inside and took our coats, I detected an unmistakable trace of sadness in her eyes.

"They've asked to see both of you," she said, and motioned for me and Bree to go upstairs.

The first bedroom on the left was much as I remembered it, subtly scented with lavender water and warmed by a crackling fire, but there was no denying that Ruth and Louise had changed. Their cheekbones stood out sharply in their hollow faces and their skin was almost translucent. Their eyes, which had always been as bright as a thrush's, took a long time to focus after Bree and I entered the room.

I remained near the door, but Bree crossed to stand between their beds.

"Hello, Auntie Ruth and Auntie Louise," she said softly, nodding to each of them in turn. "I'm Bree, your great-grandniece."

"Of course you are," said Ruth. "You have . . ."

". . . Aubrey's eyes," said Louise. "We thought we would never see . . ."

". . . his beautiful eyes again," said Ruth. "Our brother was . . ."

". . . so handsome," said Louise, with a little sigh. "Perhaps a bit too handsome . . ."

". . . for his own good," said Ruth.

If Bree was confused by their unique manner of speech, she didn't show it. She turned her head from side to side with great composure, then paused until she was sure they'd finished speaking.

"I never met my great-grandfather," she said, "but rumor has it that he was a bit of a rat."

I gazed at her in horror, but to my astonishment, both Ruth and Louise emitted wheezy chuckles.

"He was a naughty boy," Ruth acknowledged. "But he had a good heart . . ."

". . . to go along with his good looks," said Louise. "Papa told us we were mistaken in him . . ."

". . . and perhaps we were," said Ruth, "but we loved him all the same. Rumor has it . . ."

". . . that you have tattoos," said Louise.

"May we see them?" the sisters chorused.

Bree looked so thoroughly disconcerted that I had to turn away to hide my grin. Ruth and Louise seemed to be stimulated rather than abashed by their outspoken great-grandniece. They didn't need my help to handle Bree.

"We knew a sailor who had an anchor tattooed across his chest," said Ruth, "and a farmhand . . ."

". . . who had a naked lady on his biceps," said Louise. "But we've never seen tattoos . . ."

". . . on a young woman," said Ruth. "Is it the fashion nowadays?"

"Tats are, um, fairly popular in New Zealand," Bree said, folding her arms self-consciously.

"The Maori influence, I expect," said Ruth. "The peoples of the South Pacific have always had . . ."

". . . such a creative way of expressing their spiritual beliefs," said Louise. "Though it is, I believe . . ."

". . . rather more painful than flower arranging," said Ruth. "Your middle name, Aroha, is . . ."

". . . a Maori word, is it not?" said Louise.

"It is," said Bree. "Aroha is the Maori word for *love*. It was my mother's idea. She liked the sound of it."

"And the meaning, I suspect," said Ruth. "You carry with you a reminder of your mother's love . . ."

". . . wherever you go," said Louise. "And now love has entered . . ."

". . . our home," said Ruth. "Do show us . . ."

". . . your tattoos," Louise coaxed.

Bree sighed resignedly, then pushed her sleeves up to her elbows and held out her arms to allow Ruth and Louise to examine her body art.

"Splendid," said Ruth. "I see a bamboo orchid . . ."

". . . and red mistletoe," said Louise, "and white tea tree blossoms."

The expression on Bree's face told me quite clearly that she'd never expected anyone, much less a pair of ancient and eccentric

English spinsters, to take a horticultural interest in her tattoos, but again, she rose to the occasion.

"The Maori know them as peka-a-waka, pirirangi, and kanuka," she informed the sisters, pointing to the relevant blossoms as she named them. "I have a Ruru, a morepork owl, on my left shoulder."

"Fascinating," said Ruth. "You must be . . ."

". . . fond of nature," said Louise, "and flowers in particular."

"I used to cut pictures of English gardens out of magazines," Bree admitted. "But I've never had a garden of my own."

"You do now," said Ruth. "But you must tend it . . ."

". . . only if you love it," said Louise. "And you must love it for its own sake . . ."

". . . not for ours," said Ruth. "When a gift becomes a burden . . ."

". . . it ceases to be a gift," said Louise.

"You're getting ahead of yourselves," Bree protested. "You're not gone yet."

"We will be shortly," said Ruth. "Lori?"

"I'm here," I said, stepping forward.

"Thank you," said Ruth.

"Thank you," said Louise.

It was the first time I'd heard them speak as individuals. I was so surprised, and so deeply touched, that I nearly forgot my manners, but I managed to blurt an inadequate, "You're welcome."

"Tell Will and Rob," said Ruth, "that we depend upon them . . ."

". . . to carry on our tradition," said Louise. "Finch wouldn't be Finch without . . ."

". . . a set of twins to call its own," said Ruth.

"I'll tell them," I promised.

"Bree is a clever girl," Ruth continued. "If she stays on, and if she chooses to cultivate her mind . . ."

". . . as well as our garden," said Louise, "you must help her . . ."

". . . to attend university," said Ruth. "We hear there's quite a good one . . ."

". . . not too terribly far from here," said Louise.

"Oxford's not too shabby," I agreed, smiling. "Don't worry. If Bree wants my help with anything, she'll have it."

"Lori is a woman of her word, Bree," said Ruth. "If you need assistance of any kind . . ."

". . . you can rely on her to provide it," said Louise, "even if it means leaving her family . . ."

". . . and traveling to the ends of the earth," said Ruth.

"I'd do it all over again, if you asked me to," I said.

"We won't," said Ruth. "You have brought our treasure . . ."

". . . home to us," said Louise. "We hope you'll forgive us, Lori, but we would like . . ."

". . . to be alone with our great-grandniece for a while," said Ruth. "Would you please ask Nell . . ."

". . . to bring up soup and sandwiches?" said Louise. "And perhaps some . . ."

". . . seed cake," said Ruth. "The poor child needs . . ."

". . . feeding up," said Louise.

I left the Pym sisters to dote on Bree, to plan for her future, to learn as much as they could about a girl they already loved. I left them basking in the auntly pleasures that had for so long been denied them, and as I closed the bedroom door, I caught a glimpse of their identical lips curving into identical smiles.

It was the last time I ever saw those smiles.

Twenty

uth Violet Pym and Louise Rose Pym died the day after I returned from New Zealand. They passed away on a golden October evening, in the house that had always been their home, with the vicar, Nell, and Kit watching over them, and their great-grandniece holding their hands.

St. George's Church wasn't big enough to hold everyone who attended the funeral. Mourners came from miles around, filling the church and the churchyard and spilling into the lane. Though heavy gray clouds blocked the sun, those who'd brought umbrellas weren't forced to use them. The autumn rain showed its respect for the occasion by taking the day off.

Theodore Bunting, the vicar of St. George's, had prepared for a larger than usual service by attaching loudspeakers to the bell tower, but since the only speakers he could afford made him sound like a mouse with a head cold, I was glad to be seated indoors.

The villagers had, of course, arrived in plenty of time to claim their regular spots, though a few had been displaced by the pall-bearers, who sat upright and somber in the front pew. My family sat in the front pew as well, in part because Bill was a pallbearer, but mostly because Bree had asked us to sit with her. Will and Rob were torn between peering speculatively at the matching coffins and staring openly at Bree's nose ring, but for once they kept their comments to themselves. I breathed a silent prayer of thanks for the blessing of self-control.

Bree, who was the subject of much speculation in the village as well as many curious glances in the church, sat on my right, at the end of our pew, near the center aisle. She had, unbeknownst to me, spent some of our snow day in Queenstown purchasing black suede ankle boots, a black miniskirt, and a clinging black sweater that concealed her tattoos but didn't quite cover her tummy. Her youthful take on funeral attire set her apart from the rest of the mourners, as did her piercings, which, as Holly had observed, were on permanent display. When whispers began to swirl through the church, her expression became increasingly pugnacious, but she, like my boys, exercised praiseworthy self-restraint and said nothing.

The two coffins that rested side by side before the altar were indistinguishable, save for the mounds of flowers that covered them. I had an especially soft spot for the children's bouquets, if only because there were so many of them. It seemed fitting that the honorary aunts should thus be honored.

The whispering stopped when the vicar ascended the pulpit to read New Testament verses the Pyms had selected. When he invited Miss Aubrey Aroha Pym to say a few words, Bree stood without hesitation and marched over to plant herself boldly between the coffins.

"You don't know me and I don't know you," she began in a strong, clear voice. "I look strange and I sound strange and I come from a faraway place, but you'd better get used to me, because I'm not going anywhere. I promised my great-grandaunts that I'd stand in for them at a wedding in the spring, so you're stuck with me until then and maybe for a lot longer.

"Auntie Ruth and Auntie Louise weren't bothered by my looks or by my accent, and they didn't care where I came from," she continued. "I didn't know them for much more than a day, but sometimes that's all it takes to see into a person's heart. Their hearts were pure gold. I don't know whether I believe in God and I don't have much use for religion—sorry, Vicar—but if heaven exists, I know they're up there. And if there's such a thing as a guardian angel, then I have two of the best.

"Oh, and before I forget," she added, "if you want the jams and the cordials and the calf's foot jelly and the other things my great-grandaunts put by for you, you'd better come to the house to pick them up because I don't have a car and I don't know where any of you live." She brushed her hands lightly over the coffins' topmost blossoms and concluded gruffly, "Your turn, Vicar."

The whispers began again at an elevated volume as Bree returned to her pew but ceased when Theodore Bunting cleared his throat, drew himself up to his full and considerable height, and regarded his flock through narrowed eyes.

"Many people who live to a ripe old age die alone," he told us, "not through any fault of their own, but because they have outlived their friends and their family. Ruth and Louise Pym, however, never lost the knack of making new friends, and they treated each new friend as member of their family." His stern gaze came to rest on Peggy Taxman as he stated portentously, "We would do well to follow their example."

Peggy, who had been scowling disapprovingly at Bree's choppy haircut, must have felt the vicar's eyes on her because she looked up at him suddenly, turned beet-red, and buried her face in her hymnal.

The vicar, having made his point, went on. "There are those here among us today who may be angry with God for depriving us of such good and kindly souls. To them Ruth and Louise would undoubtedly say, 'Don't be silly. It's high time the dear Lord took us to His bosom, and we're quite ready to join Him, thank you very much.' They lived long and meaningful lives and they left this earth well prepared to meet their Maker. I believe steadfastly that they are at this very moment planting flowers round the gates of Heaven and greeting each new arrival with a cup of tea."

The vicar paused to spread a sheet of lined paper atop his notes.

"In closing, I will read a message Ruth and Louise asked me to convey to each and every one of you." He smoothed the sheet of paper, then read aloud, " 'Dear friends and neighbors. If you fail to show our great-grandniece the same loving kindness you have always shown us, we will smite you.' "

There was a moment of absolute silence followed rapidly by a variety of sounds. Bill and I had to bite our lips to keep from laughing out loud, but Peggy Taxman huffed indignantly, Sally Pyne tittered, and Mr. Barlow burst into a hearty guffaw. While a wave of poorly suppressed laughter rolled through the church, Rob and Will asked what "smite" meant and Bree demonstrated by giving her own knee a resounding smack.

"Let us rise," intoned the vicar. "Please turn to Hymn 457: 'For the Fruits of His Creation.' We will honor Ruth Pym and Louise Pym not merely by singing their favorite hymn, but by inscribing its words on our hearts. Let us learn from the example set by our sisters in Christ to be grateful for God's gifts, to do His will by helping our neighbors, and to recognize the good in all men."

Voices filled the church, rang out over the village, and rebounded from the surrounding hillsides as the congregation sang the old harvest hymn, reaching a crescendo in the final verse:

For the wonders that astound us,
For the truths that still confound us,
Most of all, that love has found us,
Thanks be to God.

I closed the hymnal and gazed at Bree, wondering if she'd caught the allusion the Pyms had surely known was there. Love had found them in the nick of time, I thought, filling their hearts for a few shining hours and allowing them to truly rest in peace. Thanks be to God.

"Everyone stayed for the burial," I said. "The churchyard was so packed that Mr. Barlow had to string Day-glo flags around the graves to keep people from falling into them."

Night had come and the rain had resumed. Bill, the boys, and Willis, Sr., were upstairs and asleep. Although I was dazed by a debilitating bout of jet lag, I couldn't rest until I'd told Aunt Dimity about the Pym sisters' funeral. I hadn't forgotten that they'd been her oldest friends on earth.

I sat in the tall leather armchair before the hearth in the study, with the blue journal propped open on my knees. Reginald, flanked by the pair of adorable kiwis I'd bought in Queenstown for Will and Rob, seemed content to be back in his special niche in the bookshelves, but a dreamy gleam in his eyes told me that a part of him was still roving the Land of the Long White Cloud. I smiled at him, then looked down at the familiar handwriting that had appeared on the journal's blank page.

Was the luncheon equally well attended?

"Villagers only at the luncheon," I reported, "and they couldn't complain about the food, because they'd prepared it. Bree made the most of her resources and served the casseroles and the soups well-wishers had dropped off when her great-grandaunts first fell ill. Horace Malvern's cheeses went over big."

The girl has an admirably practical turn of mind. Ruth and Louise would have approved of her economies.

"Will and Rob are positively gaga over Bree," I said. "They cornered her at the luncheon to ask little-boy questions about her nose ring and she came straight out and told them that the hole was too small to allow for . . . leakage. You should have seen Peggy Taxman's face when the boys explained it to her. I could feel Ruth and Louise smiling down on their successors."

What was the general mood at the luncheon?

"Reminiscent," I replied, after a moment's thought. "Everyone recalled something the Pyms had done for them, whether it was teaching them to make marmalade or embroidering their child's christening gown. And there isn't a gardener within fifty miles of Finch who hasn't grown plants from cuttings the Pyms passed on to them. Mr. Barlow came out with the gem of the day, though."

Do tell.

"He said, and I quote: 'It's a good thing they packed it in before the ground froze. It's hard graft, digging up frozen dirt. But they were always considerate that way.'"

Truer words were never spoken, both about the difficulty of digging graves in winter and about the Pyms' unwavering thoughtfulness.

"Nell told me that they passed away peacefully," I said.

You must take some credit for their tranquility. Bree's presence was a great comfort to them. As for the rest . . . Ruth and Louise were no strangers to death, Lori. Nearly every young man they knew, including their only brother, died in the Great War. When the Second World War began, still more young men disappeared from the village, never to be seen again. Ruth and Louise buried their parents, attended countless wakes, laid out the bodies of neighbors they'd known since childhood, and held more deathbed vigils than most doctors. When Death came for them, I'm sure they greeted him as an old friend.

"I'd like to think so." I paused to listen as a gust of rain flung itself against the diamond-paned window above the old oak desk, then said, "Bree's more upset than she'll admit."

Of course she is. She spent just enough time with her great-grandaunts to realize how painful it would be to lose them. You must look after her, Lori. She is, as you were, a stranger in a strange land. You must do for her what Cameron Mackenzie did for you.

I touched my greenstone pendant and smiled.

"I'll be a good native guide," I promised. "I learned from a master."

I believe Ruth and Louise would have enjoyed their funeral.

"The villagers certainly did," I said. "They were a lot more cheerful than I expected them to be. I thought the funeral would cast a pall over Finch."

It did, but the shadow is passing. Bree has, of course, sped the recovery process by giving the villagers something new to talk about, and Kit and Nell have done their part by giving them something to look forward to.

"A May wedding," I said, "to allow a decent interval for mourning."

After the mourning, life will go on. And what better way is there to celebrate life than with a wedding?

Twenty-one

The hedgerows were covered with supple young leaves that hid dozens of newly made nests. Bumblebees hovered over fresh clumps of clover in lush pastures dotted with lambs. The first crop of silage was ready for mowing, the rape fields were ablaze with gaudy yellow blossoms, and there wasn't a cloud in the soft blue sky as I drove Willis, Sr., to St. George's Church on a beautiful morning in May.

My father-in-law and I were alone in the car because Bill, as best man at the wedding, had left early for Anscombe Manor to lend his support to the groom. Will and Rob had gone ahead with him to prepare their ponies for the wedding procession. They and the other members of their prize-winning junior gymkhana team would escort the orange-blossom-bedecked white carriage in which the bride and her father would make the short journey from the manor house to the church.

"Lori," Willis, Sr., said suddenly, "I have made a decision."

"It's too late to change your tie again, William," I said, "and I don't know why you'd want to. We agreed—after *much* trial and error—that the pearl-gray one was perfect."

"My decision is unrelated to sartorial matters," he informed me loftily.

"Good," I said, with grim determination. "Because we're not turning around."

"I have decided to buy Fairworth House," he said.

I hit the brakes to keep from swerving into a hedge. The maneuver put no one's life at risk because our lane was the exact opposite of a major highway and Willis, Sr., had braced himself for a reaction he'd apparently anticipated. When the car came to a full stop, I rounded on him and babbled incoherently for several seconds.

"When did you . . . ? Why haven't you . . . ? You . . . buy . . . *what?*"

"Fairworth House," he replied calmly. "The ancestral home of the Fairworthy family. It is situated——"

"I *know* where Fairworth House is," I interrupted. "It's within spitting distance of Finch. I thought the place was derelict."

"It is in need of refurbishment," Willis, Sr., acknowledged, "but I should be able to move into it by the end of August. I hope you will permit me to stay at the cottage until then. I would like to be on hand to oversee the work."

"*Of course* you can stay at the cottage," I exclaimed, and leaned over to give him a hug. "Oh, William, this is the best news I've heard in ages. Bill and the boys will go crazy when they find out. Why didn't you wait until we were all together to make your announcement?"

"I learned only a few hours ago that my negotiations had been successful," he explained. "My son and my grandsons are playing vital roles in what you have on numerous occasions called the fairy-tale wedding of the century. I did not wish to distract them from their duties."

"But . . . why now?" I asked. "We've been trying to persuade you to move here since . . . forever. What changed your mind?"

"If Ruth and Louise Pym taught me anything," he said, "it is that life—even a life that lasts for more than a hundred years—is short. I intend to spend what time is left to me with those I love."

I beamed at him, restarted the car, and smiled all the way to

St. George's Church, where I, along with every other lady on the guest list, armed myself with a dainty but serviceable hanky. The men, though they would have denied it, used bandannas or pocket squares, depending on the nature of their formal attire.

It is an inarguable fact that more tears were shed at the wedding than at the funeral. Cameron, I knew, would have appreciated the irony, but I suspected that even he would have needed a handkerchief had he seen Nell gliding weightlessly down the aisle on Derek's arm.

She seemed to bring her own light with her into the church. Her veil floated like a silvery mist around her halo of golden curls, and her gown was a gossamer dream of silk beaded with seed pearls and bordered with wisps of breathtakingly delicate lace. Her eyes shone like midnight-blue sapphires and her flawless oval face glowed with a love so pure that it should have made angels sing.

As she drifted past me I saw something of the Pym sisters in the tiny honeybees they'd embroidered in white along the edge of her veil. Their industrious hands had rarely been at rest during their lifetimes, and they'd beautified everything they'd touched. They would have been pleased right down to the toes of their sensible shoes to see their ethereal creation worn by a young woman they'd loved so dearly.

The fairy princess had become the fairy queen, and her chosen king was waiting for her. Kit stood at the altar rail, with his violet eyes fixed blissfully on Nell, freed at last by her radiance from the shadows of the past that had haunted him. The connection between the two shining souls was so strong it was almost palpable. They stood side by side before the vicar to say their vows, and when Kit lifted Nell's veil and touched his lips to hers, the rapturous sighs that swept through the church nearly extinguished the altar candles.

There was much nose blowing and eye wiping, by men as well as women, as the happy couple made the return trip up the aisle, but merriment prevailed when we showered them with birdseed—which, according to the vicar, was more ecologically sound than rice—and applauded the carriage as it and its mounted escort clip-clopped jauntily away from the church.

Bill, Willis, Sr., and I paused to pay our respects to the Pym sisters before we drove to the reception. The twin graves were awash with fragrant spring blossoms and marked with one headstone into which had been carved the sisters' favorite verse from the Bible. They'd chosen a simple and well-known verse that, I believed, reflected their greathearted view of the cosmos.

GOD IS LOVE;

AND HE THAT DWELLETH IN LOVE

DWELLETH IN GOD,

AND GOD IN HIM.

—JOHN IV:16

"And here comes Aroha herself," I murmured, smiling as Bree approached.

Bree had spent most of the winter reading the gardening books she'd inherited from her great-grandaunts and discussing the contents with Emma. She couldn't have learned more about the subject if she'd taken a graduate course in horticulture at Oxford. She'd planted the snowdrops, crocuses, daffodils, and primroses that had bloomed on the Pym sisters' graves.

Bree had also bought an inexpensive used car from Mr. Barlow, who'd taken a shine to her, and spent time exploring the countryside on her own. She seemed intent on settling in for the long haul, which was, in my opinion, a good thing. I couldn't wait to see what she would do with her great-grandaunts' gardens. I somehow doubted that she'd replace their old-fashioned flowers with a practical but dull swathe of lawn.

Will and Rob still found her exotic and intriguing, as did the villagers. She'd fulfilled my expectations and outraged Peggy Taxman's sensibilities by wearing a slinky fuschia tank dress to the wedding, displaying in one fell swoop her tattoos, her feminine curves, and her shapely legs, which the Sciaparelli boys seemed to think was a *very* good thing. Bree derived immense pleasure from getting up Peggy's nose and did so fearlessly and as often as possible.

She swaggered over to straighten Willis, Sr.'s pocket square and to call an ebullient hello to Auntie Ruth and Auntie Louise. After dusting birdseed from their headstone, she followed us to the reception, where she presented the bride and groom with a gift on behalf of her late benefactresses.

"It may be a little premature," she said. "Then again, it may not."

The cheeky meaning behind her mysterious words became clear when Nell opened the box and held up an exquisitely embroidered christening gown for all to see. Nell's musical laughter filled the air while Kit, blushing furiously, hastened to assure the crowd of extremely attentive onlookers that the gift was, indeed, premature, but nonetheless cherished.

Willis, Sr., increased everyone's joy tenfold by sharing the news he'd already shared with me. He received so many congratulatory hugs that his pearl-gray tie developed a wrinkle, but I forbade him to return to the cottage to exchange it for another. I knew from recent experience that, had he gone, we wouldn't have seen him again for hours.

Kit and Nell left for their honeymoon at half past eight. No one knew where they were going, but I was certain that, wherever they went, they would find paradise. After the big sendoff, Willis, Sr., repaired to the cottage to spend the rest of the evening ironing his tie and reading quietly in front of the fire.

Bill and I tucked a drooping Will and Rob into bed at the manor house, danced until midnight, and sat up until the wee hours with Emma and Derek, sharing memories of love's first blossoming and hopes for the newlyweds' future.

I didn't have a chance to speak with Aunt Dimity until late the next day.

Epilogue

"*D*imity?" I said, gazing in triumph at the blue journal. "I've sold Bill on a family trip to New Zealand!"

Aunt Dimity's response was swift and jubilant.

Bravo! Well done! How on earth did you manage it?

"You won't believe it, Dimity." I hunkered down in the tall leather armchair in the study and gave Reginald a meaningful glance. "I hit him with the hard sell, right? I told him that Cameron and Donna are dying to meet Will and Rob. I told him that New Zealand combines the tropical beauty of Hawaii with the cozy beauty of Ireland and the alpine beauty of Switzerland. I told him that the country is the same size as Colorado but that it has more coastline than the contiguous United States. I told him about the fantastic people, the untainted food, the superb wines, the pristine environment, and I threw in the bit about hiking with fantails. And do you know what finally sold him?"

I can't imagine.

"Frodo's jacuzzi," I said.

You jest.

"Nope," I said. "I had no idea that Bill was a rabid Tolkien fan until fireworks popped in his eyes when I mentioned *Frodo's bathtub*. Can you believe it?"

Mysterious are the ways of men.

"You can say that again," I agreed fervently. "My husband, the Ringer. Who knew? I'm just happy that something clicked with him. I can't wait to go back."

Nor can I. I also look forward to William taking up residence in Fairworth House. The place has an interesting history.

"I plan to throw him the biggest housewarming party Finch has ever seen," I said. "And I won't have to prepare a single mouthful of food."

The widows of Finch will provide.

"He'll weigh three hundred pounds by next year if he's not careful," I said. "They're more eager than Bill and I are for William to move in. But no one's more excited about it than Will and Rob. They've already asked Grandpa if his new house will have stabling for their ponies."

What did he say?

"He drove them over to show them the progress that's been made in restoring the old stable to its former glory," I said. "Doting doesn't begin to describe it."

Grandfathers are, I believe, obliged by law to spoil their grandchildren.

"William is nothing if not law-abiding," I said, laughing.

Bree, too, is making progress.

"She's a breath of fresh air," I said. "She seems to know instinctively who she can razz and who deserves to be treated with respect."

I would guess that Peggy Taxman falls into one category, while the vicar falls into another.

"You've got the general idea," I said. "She's called for an economic summit with Fortescue Makepeace. She, unlike her great-grandaunts, wants a thorough explanation of her finances."

Naturally. Let us not forget that Bree was her family's accountant. She kept her father and grandfather afloat when, by rights, they should have been shipwrecked. I have no doubt that Mr. Makepeace will enjoy working with someone who understands the importance of financial security.

"They share an interest in fashion as well," I said. "She'll be as impressed by his waistcoats as he will be by her body art." I fell silent for a moment, lost in thought. "I wish Ruth and Louise were still here. They would have loved to see how well Bree's doing. They would have adored the wedding. They would have been overjoyed to see the old Fairworth place come back to life, and to have William as a neighbor. I miss them, Dimity. I wish they were here."

They are here, my dear. Their spirits bloom in gardens throughout the length and breadth of England. They can be seen in stitches embroidered for babies and brides. They live on in recipes that will be handed down for as long as berries ripen and bees make honey. Ruth and Louise are all around you, Lori. You just have to know where to look.

"I'll keep my eyes open, Dimity," I said, and as the curving lines of royal-blue ink faded from the page, the air was filled with the subtle fragrance of lavender water.

Donna's Anzac Biscuits

Makes 18–25 medium cookies

Preheat oven to 325 degrees Fahrenheit. Line two baking sheets with parchment paper.

1 cup rolled oats
1 cup all-purpose flour
1 cup desiccated coconut
1 cup sugar
4 teaspoons golden syrup or honey
½ cup butter
2 tablespoons boiling water
1 teaspoon baking soda

Place oats, flour, coconut, and sugar in a large bowl. Mix well. In a small saucepan over low heat combine the butter and the golden syrup (or honey) and heat until the butter is melted. Combine the baking soda and the boiling water and add to the butter mixture, then add the wet mixture to the dry ingredients. Mix well. Drop the dough by rounded tablespoons onto baking sheets lined with parchment paper. Bake for 12 minutes or until firm. Cool on wire racks. Munch contentedly with a nice cup of tea.